PRETTY FLY FOR A VAMPIRE GUY

A CREEPIN U STORY

LESLIE MCADAM

CD RACHELS

To J. You're pretty fly.

ABOUT THIS BOOK

Clay

I suck at being a vampire—literally. When the Halloween Wave turned a third of the population into monsters, I thought I was one of the lucky ones. I get to have my fit twenty-year-old body for decades. And vampires are supposed to be sexy, right?

But now that I'm finally in university, I still don't fit in. I was supposed to find myself and spread my metaphorical vampire wings. Yet, I'm not good enough to be an academic, and too inept at flying to hang with monsters like me. At least flirting with my new nerdy lab partner can be some fun in the meantime.

Owen

I can't stand my lab partner. It's not because he's a monster—far from it, I find vampires attractive. But jocks don't go for academics like me, especially airheads like Clay. We only need to get through this class.

Then one day, we're nursing an injured bat together, and Clay's sweet, compassionate side rears its teeth. Despite my best efforts, this gorgeous bloodsucker has me enchanted. When he wants to learn to fly, how can I refuse? This jock keeps failing at taking to the sky, but I fear I'm the one that's falling. A nerdy human like me dating a himbo vampire could spell a monster-sized disaster.

Pretty Fly for a Vampire Guy *is a spicy paranormal romantic comedy set in the Creepin U shifter universe. Don't read if you're not interested in nerd-jock connections, flying lessons through the forest, monsters at university, and yes, a happily ever after.*

CHAPTER
ONE

CLAY

Tonight is going to be fang-tastic!

I'm beaming as I wait in line with my water polo teammates outside of Zomb-Bar in downtown Creelin. It's a blustery Saturday night in January. The queue overwhelmingly consists of students—both human and monster—and stretches around the block. Everyone is laughing, chatting, and kicking at the sticky, gum-riddled sidewalk—me included. I'm moving about in excitement, good-naturedly shoving my friends, who are also all smiles.

The bouncer unhooks the purple velvet rope to allow a group of revelers to pass, and the security troll opens the bar door. One step closer! Loud music spills out onto the street.

The noise startles some bats that were hanging out in a belfry of the gothic brick church across the way, and they rise in formation, flapping their wings erratically. As their dark forms pass across the light of the full moon, my ribs squeeze tight.

"Check them out," I say to Brandon Fernandez, my best friend. "They're so awesome!"

He squints. "They look slightly drunk."

"That's because they echolocate," I say. I wish I could fly like them. I swallow hard, then paste on a wide grin. Tonight's still gonna be a scream.

Our group of ten or so shuffles closer to the front, almost everyone bundled up to protect against the icy gusts. It's as cold as my skin tonight, maybe colder. To me, it's balmy, so I'm just in a thin jacket, T-shirt, and jeans.

Bran smiles broadly and waves his phone in his gloved hand toward all of us like we don't all have our own devices. He appears comfy in his parka. "It only took fifteen minutes to get in! That's super-fast."

Ah, precious human. I bump his shoulder. Brandon's on the water polo team with me, and last summer, we bonded over complaining about two-a-day sessions. He's hot, all messy dark hair and tanned skin. But oddly, despite how gorgeous Brandon is—and how all the monsters at Creepin U want to bang him—I'm not attracted to him, and I can't explain why. Maybe it's as simple as: I normally go for bookish guys. Or girls. Or nonbinary people, since I'm not picky about gender. I do tend to favor humans, though, because OMG, have you smelled their blood? It's delish.

Sorry, I digress.

Brandon throws an arm around his boyfriend, the nøkk, who snuggles into him. The nøkk has a real name, and after the events of our water polo game against Shuford, we all know it, but none of us use it because it can kill him. That's a serious enough reason to just call him Steve.

Steve's Norwegian and currently in his human form, which makes him look like an emo teenager circa 2004: green-black hair hanging in his fully black eyes, pale greenish skin, leather jacket, band T-shirt and skinny jeans with combat boots. Steve spends plenty of time in his monster form these days, but he's a shapeshifter, and sometimes, shapeshifters gotta shift their shape. He doesn't talk much, he just gazes at Bran adoringly. He's pretty sweet, though, even if nøkk tend to be melancholy.

"I can't believe we're actually *waiting in line* to get into Zomb-Bar," Ren groans, yawning like he's bored already. Of course, he probably is. "This is Pennsylvania, not NYC."

"It's still cool," I say. Why am I older than these guys and still not jaded?

He shrugs. "Maybe."

"We're up!" Brandon chirps. Now that he's twenty-one, he eagerly shows his ID to the bouncer, and the rest of my friends pass through. Then it's my turn.

"May I see some identification?" The bouncer steps in front of me and crosses his arms over his beefy chest. Merfolk swim all up and down his arm in the form of colorful tattoos, so I'm guessing he's a merman, but I haven't seen him in the pool.

"Sure thing, hot stuff." I give him a flirty wink as I reach back to fish my wallet out of the back pocket of my jeans.

Except I have no wallet.

Shit.

What did I do with it?

I pat my pockets—all of them, including the ones inside my jacket. I have my phone, but no wallet.

Dammit.

"Don't tell me you left your wallet in your dorm room," Bran says from just beyond the purple rope, rolling his eyes.

I'd take offense at his assumption except, okay, yeah. This is pretty much on brand for me.

I smile at the bouncer, flashing my fangs. "Why does this shit always happen to me? Oh my monster god, can you believe it? I seem to have left my ID in my dorm room." I give him a conspiratorial shoulder nudge. "Trust me, I'm old enough." I start to move past him.

3

"You're Creelin U?" he asks, impersonating a brick wall, arms still crossed.

"I'm enrolled as a student, yep."

He shakes his head. "No identification, no entrance." He looks over my shoulder. "*Next.*"

I press my lips together. This is not happening.

I hate my real age, and I never like pulling out my ID, even when I have it on me. I prefer to use my inverse fake ID more often than not. It shows my age from before the Halloween Wave.

But...I want to hang with my friends. I pout. Pushing my hands together like I'm praying, I get up close to him. "Dude, I'm legal. I swear."

The entire water polo team nods from behind the rope.

"He's sensitive about his age," Brandon says.

"He's practically geriatric," Ren adds.

"That's not helpful," I sniff.

Bran taps on the enormous bouncer's shoulder, which is a bold move for anyone but Bran. "He really is older than he looks."

The bouncer points to a sign behind him that says, *If you look under thirty be prepared to show valid identification, all species, no exceptions,* and gestures to the couple behind me to come forward.

"Dude, seriously? I hate telling people my real age, but I'll do it if I need to. I'm forty years old," I blurt.

"Uh-huh. Then you should be able to show me identification. Next."

Brandon calls to me, "Cannon, dude, just go back to the dorms and get your ID. Want us to come with you?"

I shake my head. "I can do it. I'll be quick."

"Because you're a vampire and can fly, right?" Ren says.

"Something like that," I mutter. "I'll go get it. Don't wait for me, it won't take long. Go on in." I make a shooing motion at Brandon and the nøkk. Ren heads on in, following the rest of our group.

"If you're sure," Bran says, sounding uncertain. He shifts his weight from one foot to the other and huddles further into his coat.

"It's fine." I force a smile. "Go get warm. I'll be just a moment."

With one last look at me, Brandon steps inside with Steve.

I turn away from the bar and walk past downtown, headed to the forest that's between Creelin and the university. The Lin and Cree Rivers meet here, and on a warm summer day, it's downright pleasant.

Tonight it's as black as a bat cave. Good thing I have superior sight and hearing.

I use my vampire speed to race to Karloff Hall in a third of the time it would take a human to walk, and take the stairs up to my room.

Except, I forgot my key. Again. I try the handle, then pound on the door.

"Please, Yuki," I grumble. "Please be there."

No response. I can't sense any movement inside. It sounds like there's a large party going on down the hall, but getting my key is probably more important. Probably.

I sigh. I need to find our resident advisor. I return downstairs, headed to the RA's room on the first floor. To get there, I have to go through the common room, and to do that, I'm now realizing I have to pass by the most annoying people in the world: the Vampire Gliding Enthusiasts.

Shit.

I freeze, but it's too late. They've spotted me. "Well, hello, Clay Cannon," Raymond says, beckoning me closer. Ray's a senior with short black hair, smooth dark skin with bluish undertones, and vibrant purple eyes. His fangs are particularly pronounced tonight.

"Hey guys, what's up?" I shove my hands in my pockets.

"We were just discussing membership," Shannon says.

Her hair's dyed red, but I'm not sure what color it really is. She also has dark skin, but it's not as blue as mine or Raymond's. Maybe she just ate. Or maybe she's wearing makeup.

I glance up, and they're looking at me expectantly. Guess I got distracted by whether Shannon's wearing makeup or not. "Sorry?"

"We want all of the vampires on campus involved in our club so we can have some proper fun."

"Fun," I repeat, doing my best to sound enthusiastic. "I'm all for fun."

"You'll have to join us on our big field trip in a month. We're going gliding in the Poconos!"

"Sounds terrific." I back my way out of the room. "Sorry, but I need to talk to the RA. I'm locked out of my room."

"Very well. We'll see you at our next meeting in a week, Clay! Don't miss it!" Shannon chirps.

"Sure thing." I flee down the hall and pound on the RA's door. He helps me get into my room, where my keys and wallet are right where I left them. I grab them and shove them in my jeans so I can head back to Zomb-Bar.

Am I the most forgetful vampire who ever lived? Likely so.

But the worst thing about me?

I can't fly.

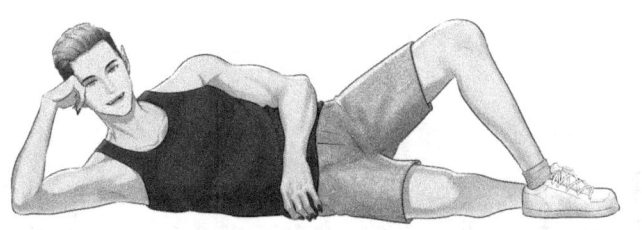

CHAPTER

TWO

OWEN

I click my laptop and the large screen before me flicks to the next slide. We're gazing at a collage of photos I compiled from the internet, now on the dorm flatscreen TV. There're dozens of vampire dude selfies, all shirtless pecs, smooth blue-gray skin, tight abs, and the occasional set of fangs. *Yum.*

I glance down at my tablet and read my notes. "Vampires have super-strength, making them strong protectors. More importantly, they're virile, meaning they can last long in bed."

This earns me a chuckle from my peers sitting before me in my friend's suite. I push up my glasses and swipe to my next page of notes. "Some people are afraid of their retractable fangs, but I'm not. I think kissing one would be a fascinating change of pace. With enough trust, a vampire sucking blood from you could be an intimate experience. Consensually, of course."

I click, and the next slide reveals a vampire leaping out of a pool. Water splashes everywhere, framing his muscly abs in the sexiest way. I try not to drool at the photo that I downloaded from the school website and clear my throat. I had the forethought to cover the guy's face with our school logo—for privacy, naturally.

"Vampires also age slower than humans. So dating one means you have a strapping young stud for years to come." Everyone laughs, and I click one last time to show a dark slide that reads, *Thank You.*

"We've all had to deal with major life changes since the Halloween Wave morphed so many of us into shifters twenty years ago. When it comes to interpersonal relations, we simply have to overcome our preconceived notions to unite monsters and humans. As such, I believe I have more than convinced you that vampires make ideal boyfriends. While I accept all monsters, as a human, I would be more than happy to date a vampire." I look up and slightly bow. "Thank you for your time. I will now be taking any questions."

The small audience stares at each other in silence for a moment. Then, a hand raises.

"Yes, Tanner?" I point to my closest male friend.

"Yeah, um, why did you insist on showing us your little dog and pony show?" He cringes and exchanges perplexed looks with the others. We all appear to be ordinary human under-grads, but I know Tanner's boyfriend is a monster. There are some other faces I don't recognize sitting in chairs or on the floor.

"Not that this wasn't, um...interesting." My closest female friend, Shonda, smirks and nudges the dude next to her. "But we didn't ask for a lecture. Even though it was very revealing, Owen. High marks."

They all laugh, and I frown. "You asked me to come over," I reply.

"Yeah, to have drinks before the start of the spring semester," Rachel, my other human friend, points out. "Maybe play some games. Not listen to you wax poetic about how to objectify vampires."

"I was not...objectifying vampires," I retort as my cheeks heat up.

"Wasn't there one slide showing a vampire's backside and a peach emoji?" Kovi asks. His boyfriend, Tanner, giggles and bumps his shoulder into him, then they both sip their beers.

I clear my throat. "I was trying to prove that I'm not opposed to dating certain monsters." I look away out the dorm window. As usual, no one understands my research.

"Well, I liked it. A-plus work, bro." Seth points at me and leans against the wall. Our resident mummy is in his human form. He drinks from a beer bottle and, as always, has an easy grin on his face. I smile at him, then he adds, "Very horny. The horniest thing I've ever seen. It should be your dissertation."

Everyone chuckles, and my smile falls.

"Is this HowlerPoint presentation because I texted you over break saying how everyone should date a dryad?" Tanner asks. He grabs his boyfriend's thigh where they both sit closely on the couch. "I didn't mean to say other monsters aren't attractive."

"Thank you, kindly," Seth says, and bows, earning more laughter.

"And you didn't have to like...do a whole academic presentation," Kovi says.

"Hey, if you wanna bone a vampire, we would have believed you," Shonda adds.

Again, the whole dorm of drunk students laughs, and I frown. "This presentation is over."

Kovi stands up and announces, "Okay, now that we're done being forced to watch..." He points at the screen and grimaces. "*That*." The room snickers, and he smiles again. "Who wants to play Cards Against Monsterkind?"

"Yes! Let's do it!" Seth says. Nearly everyone cheers and huddles in a circle.

I'd be annoyed that my peers don't appreciate my presentation skills, but I'm used to it by now. Also, I don't need any more humiliation before classes have even started. Or to induce a panic attack from overthinking. So, I'm happy to step back and let my so-called friends play a fun drinking card game. I haven't fit in for the past twenty-one years of my life, why start now?

"Hey." One skinny, shorter fellow walks up to me. There are several folks I don't know personally that Kovi invited to this little dorm gathering, but I wasn't paying attention. "I noticed you took some photos from our team website."

I gulp and the blood drains from my face. He's cute, and his Scottish accent is musical. But that's not what has me in a nerdy fight-or-flight mode. "Um, they were stock photos. Of vampires and such."

"No, some of those were from the water polo team. I should know, they're my people." He looks me directly in the eye. Fortunately, everyone else seems to be enthralled by the party game on the floor.

Shit, this guy is on the team. "And that second-to-last slide was Clay."

I gulp and quickly shut off my laptop. "I...don't know what you mean. They're random shifters I pulled from Boogle and Witchipedia."

"Right, sure." He tilts his head and pauses, then sips his drink. "A bunch of my team, including Clay, went to Zomb-Bar tonight, but I heard about a dorm party and couldn't resist."

Oh, thank monster god. "Mhm!" I squeak, choosing to scrutinize my laptop bag.

"I could introduce him to you." He smirks and taps my shoulder, and I flinch away. "Like team solidarity. I'm Nick by the way."

My mouth goes dry. They say never meet your heroes, but I think that also extends to the fine water polo jock you've been lusting after since the end of last semester.

"Well, Nick." I adjust my glasses and hike my bag over my shoulder. "I wish you and the uh, water polo team much success this semester. But all of those photos were random vampires. I don't know who this Clay is."

Is he a monster that can detect lies? "And I'm not looking to meet or date anyone right now." *More lies.*

He stares at me skeptically while everyone near us laughs at the card game. "Are you sure? Because there was an entire slide detailing what your vampire-slash-Indian-human-gay wedding would be like."

I clear my throat and my shoulders tense up. "That was uh, hypothetical. Buh-bye!" I dash out of the dorm suite, not bothering to say goodbye to my friends.

I walk out of Karloff Hall and into the cold January air. Pennsylvania is freezing this time of year, but the entire Creepin U...um, I mean Creelin University campus is buzzing with excitement. The start of a new semester means new opportunities for monsters and humans to forge strong interpersonal relationships. After all, last semester was their first time letting humans in, and I was part of that inaugural batch.

As I walk past a large snake cuddling with a handsome dude on a bench, I bite back a sigh. Okay, yes, I admit I'm lonely. And more than a little starved for intimacy, hence working all night on a vampire-themed slideshow.

But everyone at the party thought it was a wacky good time. I'm not sure what's worse—my closest friends finding my research ridiculous, or a water polo jock taking it seriously and offering to introduce me to Clay Cannon. *He is one fine vampire boy...*

Shit, what if Nick tells Clay I used his picture in my lustful presentation? I'll seem like a total weirdo. I mean, I *am* a nerdy weirdo, but I don't want the hot water polo monster to know that.

I make it to my dorm building and swipe my card to get in. I relax my shoulders, then take the stairs up to my room.

It'll be fine. I can focus on classes starting in two days. It's not like I'll ever meet Clay anyway.

As I SIT in the front row of the lab classroom, I try to ignore the murmurs of fellow students walking in. Yes, I came to class early as always and managed to snag the seat closest to the professor. My human buddies aren't in this lecture-practicum-hybrid course, so I'm on my own.

That's fine; on my own is what I'm used to.

I stare at my reflection in my phone out of boredom. Just because I'm a nerdy, lonely, kind of neurotic dude, doesn't mean I don't care about how I look. I take off my glasses and study myself: my ochre skin is clear, thank monster god, and my trimmed black hair slightly curls over my forehead, just the way I like. Sure, I wish I could be defined in my belly and more bulky in my arms, but that's a problem for another day. I've never liked exercising, and therefore don't deserve a tight, athletic physique.

I am who I am, and that is certainly no jock.

The students around me lull into a hush, and I know what that means. The professor walks to the front, and I put my glasses back on. She's an older woman with a high brown pony-tail, and she's wearing a lab coat.

"Welcome everyone! Good morning!" She gives a wave and

her chipper energy forces me to sit upright at the lab bench. "So glad you were able to find the lab. Did you all print your syllabi?"

"Yes," I reply, along with a few of my fellow students behind me.

"Fang-tastic." She puts her hands together and beams at us. "I'm Professor Robinson, but please call me Octavia. I'll be yours this semester for Monster Anatomy 101." She shifts before us, her skin turning purple and her clothes disappearing into her monster skin.

The class gasps—she's a kraken shifter! Most monsters have human guises, so it's often a surprise to see their monster form. Her hands and torso look like a purple human, but as she leans forward, I know her bottom half must be tentacles.

And this is confirmed when a tentacle rises up behind her and takes a piece of chalk from the chalkboard.

"We have a lot to cover this semester, what with the dozens of species of monsters. But don't worry, I will be your creature guide." She laughs, but I can't pay attention while her tentacle writes on the board. She isn't even looking, but it manages to write the words, *Monster Anatomy*.

Fascinating. Monsters are *so* cool.

"One of the most important things you should know about this class is that we do everything in pairs." I sift through the syllabus in my hands as I listen to Professor Robinson. "And according to my census, exactly half of you are human and half are shifters. Isn't Creelin University just wonderful?"

She claps her hands and laughs. "So befriend a monster if you're human, and if you're a monster, link up with a human sitting next to you." I turn around—all the students behind me are paired up at their lab tables. A minotaur stands up and swaps with a human so now it seems everyone is in a human-monster coupling.

To my left, my table is vacant—typical, even in academics I can't find a monster to link up with.

The professor looks at my table and her smile falls. "I'm sure people are just late since this is the first day." I hear the door open behind me and the professor waves. "Right on schedule. Come to the front and have a seat, you're just in time."

She turns around and proceeds to write, tossing the chalk from her tentacle to her hand. "As I said, it's imperative to academically pair up." She begins to write words, and I sense a presence to my left.

"Sorry I'm late," the dude whispers, and a chill runs up my spine. When I turn to look at him, I swivel back to the front, then do a double take.

Oh my monster god. It's Clay Cannon. Super-hot vampire jock...*is now my lab partner?*

THREE

CLAY

W̲ell, *hello*, nerdy-sexy human. Wouldn't it be nice to sink my teeth into your neck.

Behind tortoiseshell, plastic-rimmed glasses, a brown-eyed beauty blinks at me. He has dark brown hair with a curl I want to tug on, and gorgeous, velvety, dark brown skin. He's wearing neat jeans and a buttoned-up, tucked-in plaid shirt with navy blue sneakers.

A thrill races through my body, because *damn*. He smells sweet, like maybe vanilla mixed with nutmeg. His pulse beats fast in his neck, so loudly I can hear it. My fangs pop out, and my smile slowly builds. What I wouldn't give to drink from him instead of a cold bag of O-negative from the cafeteria.

But I don't drink from humans without their consent. Or do anything else without consent.

I'd like to see what he'd let me do to him, though.

He's smaller than me, but hardly skinny. He doesn't appear to be athletic, but I don't care about that. I'd simply love to see what's under those clothes. My fingers tingle with the need to touch him. Taste him. Taste his blood.

Stop staring, Clay.

Also, stop getting ahead of yourself.

He's unabashedly studying me. Figures. I'm kind of used to that.

I hold out a hand, lowering my voice. "Clay Cannon. Sorry I was late. I left my phone in my room and had to go back for it. Then I couldn't find the classroom. Nice to meet you."

The cute man cocks his head to one side and bites his lip, studying my outstretched hand.

I frown. Everyone else in the room seems to be chatting up their neighbor.

Is there something wrong with me? Maybe he doesn't like monsters? Or vampires? Or is it just me?

My hand is its normal pale bluish color. What's going on?

I clear my throat. Finally, after what feels like hours, he shakes my hand with a firm grip. Monster god, his palm is toasty warm, and it sends a funny burst of energy up my body. "Owen Bhat. B-H-A-T."

Okay, even his voice is sexy—a little raspy, but deep and soothing.

Clapping his shoulder, I say, "Bhat man! Awesome!"

Owen juts out his jaw, his tone tart. "It's Owen. Not Bhat man."

Shit. Oops. Didn't mean to offend him. I nod a few times. "Cool, cool. Whatever you say." The professor is now staring at me, and I mime zipping my lips and face forward, slumped in the seat, my legs spread. "Sorry, professor."

"That's quite all right," she says, and the class quiets down to listen. "Now that we're settled, I'd like to go over what you can expect from this class."

Thus begins the first hour of torture from being near this beguiling human. He's sitting so tantalizingly close to me, yet so far away. I don't remember the last time I was this distracted by a human. Maybe when I was first turned?

19

Because this feeling of *want* is intolerable. Utterly intolerable.

While we're supposed to be taking notes and paying attention to the kinds of monster anatomy we're going to learn about, all I want to do is inspect a few parts of the human anatomy of the man next to me. With my tongue. And my fangs. I'm salivating.

Quit it, Clay, or you'll be giving the whole class a demonstration of what your own anatomy can do when you're aroused.

I do my best to focus on the professor, but it's hard, pun intended. The minotaur sitting behind me can probably smell my arousal and is now clued in to my predicament. Whatever.

Then the professor turns to the part of the syllabus about vampires. "We will be covering not only the parts of a vampire that are modified for blood-feeding, but the unique adaptations that allow a vampire to glide or fly along wind currents."

I stay stock still, but I want to groan. *Not this again.* When people come across monsters, they have certain expectations. Werewolves shift when there's a full moon. Merfolk swim with ease. Bird shifters are lactose intolerant. And vampires drink blood and fly.

The prof eyes me. "I'm sure we'll be able to have insightful comments from any vampires in the class."

Hesitantly, I nod and then look around. Everyone's staring at me, and it's not because of my water polo prowess.

Dammit.

But then my partner shifts in his seat so our thighs brush, and I really want to groan.

Down, boy, I tell my dick. It doesn't listen, and now I need to listen to the rest of the professor's lesson with a tent in my pants.

At the end of the lecture, Owen turns to me, but he doesn't

look me in the eye. "Um, I think we should exchange phone numbers," he mutters.

Visions flash through my mind of taking this man out on a date, then fucking him into oblivion.

Not that he's given me any indication he's interested. *Except...*

Let's review the facts: One, he's asking for my number. And two, I know he was aware of me this entire time. His breathing quickened and his skin was flushed. His tongue kept darting out to touch his lips, and he kept lifting his chin up, exposing his neck and that delicious vein.

Gah.

Owen's poking his tongue into his cheek, which isn't helping my thoughts. Oh, he's waiting for me.

"You know," he continues. "For our joint projects?"

"Yeah, I got it. Sure."

I give him a sheepish smile and recite my number while still sitting, so I can hide my erection under the desk. He texts me.

UNKNOWN NUMBER

Hey, this is Owen Bhat

My fingers hover over my phone screen to text back when my phone lets out the distinctive notification sound for WereScruff.

Shit. I hit ignore, save his name as Sexy Human Lab Partner, and text him back.

ME

Got it!

I rub the back of my neck. "See you in class, then."

"Yeah, see you." Owen grabs his bag, slings it over his shoulder, and walks off, his ass delectable in those jeans.

I shake my head slightly, then stand and adjust myself now that the class is mostly empty.

Get a grip, horndog.

POLO PRACTICE TODAY is after classes but before dinner. Water polo's winding down for the season, but we have exhibitions and scrimmages left. The Creelin pool complex is indoors, and on a snowy January day like today, the windows are extra fogged up.

In the locker room, I strip out of my clothes and tug on my extra-tight Speedo, then bang my locker closed. I don't need goggles—the salt water isn't irritating.

What *is* vaguely irritating is Nick MacGregor, the Loch Ness Monster shifter who's on the team. He grins at me. "I know something you don't know."

I huff. "What is this, first grade?"

He chuckles, his Scottish accent thicker than usual. "I went to a dorm party this weekend, and you featured heavily."

"Oh?" I grab my towel from the bench and walk with him the short distance out to the pool area. Brandon and the nøkk are already in the water, horseplaying along with a few others from the team. I love our camaraderie. "How so?"

"Aye, a certain human was giving a presentation at the party on how sexy he thought vampires were, and you were one of the examples."

I stop short, and he almost bumps into me. "Really?"

He nods. "Seems like he was very into wet, hot vampire jocks. He had a HowlerPoint Presentation and everything."

"Why on Earth was someone giving a full presentation at a party?"

Nick shrugs. "Why not? It was fun. And he definitely has a crush on you."

"This is utterly delightful. Who was the guy?" My towel goes on the bleachers, and I pad over to the water.

Nick also puts his towel down and jumps into the pool. When he comes up for air, he says, "He didn't tell me his name, but I think they said it was Owen."

Huh. That's interesting. But there has to be more than one person named Owen at this school. "What did he look like?"

"I'd call him bookish. Dark hair. Medium build. Not tall."

A smirk breaks out on my face. So my sexy little lab partner has a crush on me. Good thing for him, the feeling's mutual.

FOUR

OWEN

The Creelin University dining hall is fascinating. All of the food is monster-themed or literally tailored for monsters. When your clientele are different species, it stands to reason that you need various food groups. I plate a serving of chicken monster-sala over rice—Indian representation for the win! Next, I push my tray over and pass by the giant flanks of bloody steak and chicken and grimace. I'm no fan of raw meat, but I'm sure the werewolves love it. Incubi require sexual energy, so it would be highly entertaining if some sexual partners sat near the cafeteria lines to allow public intimacy for feeding. I snicker at the absurd thought as I fill up a cup of Ghosta Cola.

Then I imagine a certain sexy vampire in the cafeteria with me, taking off his clothes. The man is a snack after all.

I shake my head as I make it to a far corner with my meal. *No thinking of my sexy lab partner.* Water polo clearly does his body good, and sure, I've beaten off to the sight of his tight abs more than once since I first saw him at a game last semester. But so what? His athletic body is all the more reason to not make a move.

He's such an airhead he probably floats up and glides away with his vampire powers. We have nothing in common, and clearly I need to carry us this semester in Monster Anatomy.

I take a spoonful of chicken monster-sala and gaze around. Werewolves, mummies, gorgons, and golems are all paired up with various humans. They're all canoodling, eating meals, and nearly recreating that scene from *Lady and the Tramp* with pasta. I turn back around and frown, facing the window.

It's early in the semester, but almost everyone is paired up. Optimistic me thought I'd meet a monster by now who understands my nerdy ass. At least I have friends who seem to tolerate me. And through them, I get to hang out with monsters, too.

Before I can get too deep in my thoughts, a name pops up on my phone. I frown—I might as well get this over with. I swipe, and my mom's face appears on the screen. She has dark hair, ochre skin, and she peers closely into the camera.

"Beta, how are you?"

"Hi, Mom," I reply, trying to give a sincere smile.

"First you leave for that terrifying creepy school, then you don't talk to us for a week?"

I frown. "It's not a creepy school, it's Creelin U."

"But I was so afraid that one of those monsters ate you or something."

I huff and look around, confirming that no one is in earshot. Then again, vampires have super senses. "Mom, that's super offensive to monsters," I say in a hushed tone.

"You're afraid of offending monsters but not scared of offending your own parents." She moves the camera, and I spy Dad gazing at a newspaper. He has glasses on his nose, and he resembles a balding version of me, or rather, I resemble a curly-haired version of him, a trait I got from Mom. "Can you believe your son?"

Dad bristles in response, and I try not to roll my eyes on camera. I love my folks, but they're so overbearing, they make me seem normal in comparison. I may have inherited Mom's perpetual nervousness.

"Are you eating enough?" Mom's face covers the phone again. "You look so skinny."

"I'm actually eating lunch right now." I hold up a spoon in a desperate attempt to calm Mom down. "Chicken masala, actually." Mom doesn't need to know it's actually monster-sala.

She peers at my food through the screen, and I can almost feel her judgment over the dish. "Anyway, how are you doing? We worry about you, Owen."

"I know, Mom." I sip my drink. "But I'm all right."

"It's not too late to transfer to a proper human school to do pre-med."

I sigh. "I can get plenty of pre-med credits here."

Mom's gaze widens and she grimaces. "Who is that behind you?!"

I turn around and notice a lagoon monster, gills and all, holding a tray. The dude points to the salt shaker next to me, and I hand it to him.

"Thanks," the dude murmurs.

"Some guy wanted salt," I say.

"There are so many monsters there!" Mom seems genuinely distressed, looking wildly all around her room. We keep having these conversations over and over again. "Are you not fearful for your life?"

I grit my teeth. "No, Mom. They're just people who look different. We look different, too, to a lot of folks."

She purses her lips; she doesn't look convinced. "As long as you graduate in one piece and go to a respectable med school, that's all we care about."

"So I've heard," I mutter. Mom might have a heart attack if

she finds out I want to practice medicine for monsters. I love her, but I thought by now she'd be cool with me going to the infamous Creepin U.

"Beta, you know we just want you to be safe and thrive at school."

"I know." My shoulders deflate. "How is Auntie?"

Mom scoffs, then perks up; she loves talking trash about her sister, and I've managed to pivot the conversation for now.

Admittedly, I haven't accomplished what I wanted when I transferred here in the fall of my junior year. But it's a new year, a new semester—maybe all my monster academia dreams will come true this winter.

I KNOCK ON THE DOOR, and Professor Robinson looks up. "Come in!"

I take the seat across from her at her desk. There are posters on the walls of her office detailing the skeletal anatomy of mermaids and ogres. I half-expected cauldrons and other occult paraphernalia, but this just resembles a small science-lover's room. The professor is wearing a salmon-colored blouse while I'm in my puffy black winter coat. I seem to have caught her in the middle of highlighting some notes.

I put down my backpack and nod. Since it's only the second week of the year, I know her office hours are wide open.

"Hi, Professor."

"Please, it's Octavia." She waves me away, and I chuckle. I half-expected her to be in her kraken form, but no, she has hands, not tentacles at the moment.

"Right." I push my glasses up and take out a notebook. "I

wanted to pick your brain about the assignment of the semester."

"Of course. Have a seat. Monster Anatomy 101, right? Front row?"

I smile. "That's me. Owen Bhat."

"What do you got for me, Owen?" She swivels in her chair and closes her notebook.

I lean forward. "I wanted to know how hands-on we can be for the midterm project."

"An early starter." She winks and bites on her highlighter. "I like that. What were you considering, Owen?"

"Well, I was going to compare dryad branches to the human nervous system."

Her expression turns quizzical. "I don't recall having a dryad in class. Is your lab partner a tree spirit?"

My smile vanishes. "No ma'am, he's a...vampire."

"Perfect!" She leans forward and puts her hands together on her desk. "Owen, this class is about an exchange in anatomies. A lot of shifters ignore their human side. Even before the Halloween Wave shaped our world, human beings had so much to learn in the body. The skeletal system...lymph nodes..." She rolls her wrist in the air. "The list goes on and on, and I want your lab partner to explore that."

My face falls. "So, you want us to...exchange anatomy?"

"Exactly. Do research, interview each other, and get to know other species." She grins. "Did you know that vampires gain pseudo-flight with their skin and bones?"

Shifting in my seat, I push up my glasses. "I have read about it, but..."

"And what about the enzymes in their saliva to make feeding painless? Have you heard about that?"

"Not yet, no."

"There ya go!" She points at me. "There's so much to learn.

And we need future generations of anatomy experts for healthcare."

I stare down at my empty notebook, a lump in my throat. Octavia is the first person I've come across who explicitly wants me to learn about monsters, which makes sense since she's the professor. A part of me is thrilled, but another part of me is dreading growing closer to Clay.

"Go on, Owen. Take some time to link up with your vampire lab partner. You can teach him about his human side, and he can show you what vampires can really do."

I nod and pack my things. "Thanks, Pro...Octavia."

"Best of luck!" she sings, and I walk out of her office.

Passing a group of chatting Aztec mummies in the hallway, I frown, knowing I have to text that frustratingly hot himbo vampire.

THE LIBRARY IS my place of solitude. Besides the gorgon dude who works at the front desk, I get to study in peace. Multiple books are splayed about before me on the massive wooden table. Each tome details the most up-to-date information on vampire anthropology. I've done plenty of research on the internet, but, admittedly, I was distracted by their pretty faces and fangs. The blame belongs to infuriatingly sexy Clay and his tight abs.

But maybe he can help us both out. I've jotted down several bites—ha ha—of information from these books that can assist us. I've also snapshotted various charts and graphs. When I'm in my academic zone, I can absorb a ton of details.

However, Octavia thinks I should be more hands-on, and

now I have to agree. The enzymes in vampire saliva sound fascinating. I'm sure no one wants to hear me wax poetic about fang shapes, but this research is for my grade. *Our* grade—Clay needs to jump in on this.

I whip out my phone.

ME

Are you free tonight?

I continue reading one of the books in front of me. Apparently, vampire bones are light when they need to be, lending to their gliding capabilities—*this is astounding*.

When my screen lights up, I take a gander at my phone again.

CLAY

I could be.

ME

You and I have stuff to do. Mutually beneficial stuff.

CLAY

Tonight? What did you want to do?

ME

Need to get my hands on a monster, specifically a vampire.

I would love to assess your body.

And what a vampire mouth is capable of.

CLAY

Oh? I'm not NOT consenting. You don't mind if people see us?

ME

Well, ideally we'd be alone in your room, so privacy isn't an issue. Is that a good plan?

CLAY

My body is so ready.

Well, that settles that! I finish closing all my books and wave at the gorgon boy at the front desk. I hike my backpack on and stride away. Tonight is going to be a great night for knowledge and academia.

CHAPTER

FIVE

CLAY

I never thought Nerdy Hottie would be so forward, but I'm *very* okay with it.

Putting down my phone, I turn to my roommate. Yuki's been playing Monster Mash Brothers on his Nintendo-Ogre Witch console, like he does every night. It's a fighting game, and he's been swearing at it nonstop for ten minutes, so I guess whomever he's playing with online is kicking his ass. He likes to be victorious, and doesn't deal well when he's outmatched.

"Hey, uh, I got a date right now. Or maybe just a hookup. Do you mind letting me have some alone time? I'll return the favor whenever you want."

Yuki rolls his eyes. After a semester, he's used to me. He hooks up about as much as I do, so we've come to an implicit agreement of just asking for what we want and being blunt about it. No need to pretend we're doing something other than having sex. "Yeah, fine. I could stand to do some homework anyway. Text me when it's safe to come back."

I grin at him. "Thanks!"

Slipping his laptop into his messenger bag and donning a

large coat, Yuki gives me a funny little salute. Then, he heads out the door, taking his keys and phone with him.

I clap my hands once and survey the room.

Now, it's time to arrange a little better mood. I quickly fly around the room—okay, not literally fly since I can't—and use my monster speed to tidy up, throw my trash away, hang up my clothes, and make my bed. I turn off the overhead light and instead put on the bedside table lamp to really amp up the sexiness. Finally, I inspect my face in the mirror.

Yes, I can see myself in mirrors: blue-black pompadour, purple eyes, and smooth, blueish skin. I'm not sure why I bother, since I always look the same. I can't really do anything about my appearance. Even when I cut my hair, it grows back the next day to look exactly like this.

I reread the texts Owen sent, and my cock starts to swell even more. I'll *happily* show him what my *mouth is capable of*. My deepthroating is legendary. I also can't wait to feel what his hands are like when they're on me. I palm my hardening dick as I read. *Nrgh, so good*. The anticipation is killing me.

Since Owen says he wants my body, should I just be ready for him? I internally shrug. Might as well.

I tug my T-shirt over my head and shimmy off my jeans and boxer briefs. I sniff my armpits. It's an old human habit I haven't been able to shake even though I always smell fresh, clean, and seductive.

Glancing around the room, I don't see anything else to do. Yuki always turns the heat up in here, so it should be comfortable for a cute human like Owen. Will he want some water or something? Yuki won't mind if I borrow one of his bottles. Humans can get dehydrated when they have sex. I pull one out of Yuki's minifridge and set it next to the lube and tissues on the bedside table.

With nothing further to do but wait, I lie down on my bed

and arrange myself on my side, my head propped up on my hand. I glance down at my body and nod. I look good, and my cock is very excited that it's going to get a little attention from someone other than me. I think it's been a whole week since I've hooked up with someone else—that's ages.

Ten minutes later, I hear a hesitant knock on my door. My vampire senses are going haywire. There's a tasty morsel of a human right outside my room.

My voice drops to its lowest register. "Come in."

The knob twists and the door opens. Light spills in from the hallway as Owen shuffles inside.

"Hey, thanks." Owen's back is turned as he closes the door, a navy blue parka in one hand, and a messenger bag in the other. He turns around, and we lock eyes.

He freezes, and I grin. Then, his eyes roam across my body, widening behind his glasses. His mouth opens, but no words come out. I can hear his blood coursing through his veins and sense it heating his cheeks. There's the beginning of a distinct bulge in his pants. I can smell his arousal.

This is going to be fun.

Owen drops his messenger bag on the floor. "Oh, monster god," he whispers.

I wave at him. "Hey," I purr. "Come on in and get comfortable. You surprised me when you texted me, but I'm up for anything." I gesture at my stiff cock. "As you can see."

A bead of sweat shows up on his brow as he shields his eyes and turns slightly away from me. "Wha...wha...Why are you naked?" he yelps, his voice a higher register than usual.

"Um, so we can do it? Just like you texted me." I scratch my jaw.

"I did not!"

"You totally did. You said you wanted to inspect my body."

"Assess your body!"

"Same thing," I reply with a grin and a shrug. "So assess it."

"Not like that!" he sputters, his hands gesturing up and down in my general direction. His eyes are still closed, so he's really pointing more to my pillow.

I glance down again at my body. "What's wrong with it? Is... is it bad?"

There must be some hurt in my voice because he cracks one eye open and assiduously looks me in the face. "When I said I wanted to study your anatomy for class, I didn't mean that you needed to get naked."

I frown. "How else were we supposed to have sex?"

"We're not having *sex*!" Owen shrieks. He looks up at the ceiling and flails his arms about. "This is for our *grade*! I wanted to, you know, learn about how your body is different from mine. Not suck your dick!"

I look pointedly from my cock to the front of his jeans where he's already sporting a semi. "I mean, I'm noticing how our bodies are more similar than different."

He sputters and shakes his head. "This is ridiculous. Can you please put some clothes on?"

I huff and frown. "Sure," I say, chastened. I've never had anyone reject me over my body. In fact, that's the thing most people like about me. Some people say my skin's too cold, but on a hot summer day, I'm told there's nothing better. Hot sweaty sex with a vampire can be refreshing.

I stand up and walk over to my dresser, my dick bobbing in front. "Hey, I'm sorry if this is too fast for you." I pull out some athletic shorts, yanking them up my thighs. "Is this better?" I ask, my hands waving toward my chest and hips.

"Not really," he mutters. "You're still a...a total distraction." He sighs and pinches the bridge of his nose. "Clay, I need you to be my lab partner, not—" he points to me—"whatever this is you're thinking."

"You're really sure you don't want to have sex?" I ask, feeling dejected. "Because we can still do whatever it is you want to do for class. I'm just really good at blowjobs."

Owen pulls his shoulders back, chin lifting up. "I'm sure." He grabs his parka and puts the strap of his messenger bag over his shoulder. "I can't study with you today. I'll...see you in class." He turns and leaves, slamming my door behind him.

I stare at the door, wondering what the hell just happened. And why is my chest hurting?

THE NEXT MORNING, I'm going through the noisy cafeteria line with Brandon and the nøkk. I've got my usual O-negative while Bran's tray is loaded up with bacon, fruit, scare-rambled eggs, and toast. The nøkk's holding two cups of coffee, presumably one for him and one for Brandon. He's in his monster form, his gray, mottled skin showing and moss hanging off of him. The dining hall is crowded because it's snowing outside and everyone wants to stay in. A group of harpies is gossiping in the corner, and some humans are playing on their phones even though their trays are cleared away.

"You seem different," Bran remarks once we take our seats at a table. "Is something wrong?"

"I didn't have sex last night," I blurt, after taking a big sip of my breakfast blood.

Bran spits out his coffee and yelps. "What the hell, dude? I don't need to know your sex life." Steve hands him a napkin, and Bran gives him an affectionate kiss on the cheek.

My chest feels like it's caving in, and my toes curl up. I want to hide behind something. "I thought I was going to hook up with my monster anatomy partner, but I read him wrong."

The nøkk rubs his chin, his eyebrows squishing together as he frowns at Brandon. "Is sex something you often talk about with Clay?"

"Sometimes," Brandon says. Light dawns in his eyes, and he turns to me. "When he said he wanted to 'study,' you thought he meant something else."

"Yeah, I mean, isn't that what everyone means when they say they're going to study?" I bite my lip, then remember I have fangs so I don't want to do that hard. I stare down at the table, then glance up again.

The nøkk shakes his head. "In Norway, when we say we are going to study, we mean we are going to study."

"It's the same in English," Bran says to him. "Clay's just weird."

"I'm not weird!" I say indignantly. "But I'm pretty sure I just made things *very* weird with him last night. I'm wondering if he's still going to want to be my lab partner anymore. And I need to pass my classes. I don't want to waste my time here."

"Oh monster god, what did you do?" Brandon asks, amusement plain on his face.

"It doesn't matter," I mutter. "But now I can never talk to him ever again."

"That's going to be a problem if you need to work together in class," Steve says.

I sigh. "This is a monsterclusterfuck."

A FEW DAYS LATER, I'm hit with another monsterclusterfuck. I'm headed for the RA's room to get another key when the Vampire Gliding Enthusiasts all but corner me again in the common room of Karloff Hall. Yes, I lost mine again. I really should just not lock the door. But then when I don't lock up, cute humans can come barging in and make me feel like monster shit by turning down sex. With me. Like, who does that?

"Clay!" Raymond says, appearing next to me. Ugh, he's so much faster than me. It seems like he flew across the room when he likely just took a big hop.

"Hey," I say weakly. My mind scrambles as I try to come up with an excuse as to why I have to leave the dorm right this second. In a snowstorm.

"Are you able to go gliding with us?" he asks.

"I might be busy that weekend."

"You don't even know what date we're going," Shannon says, coming up behind Raymond.

Don't make me admit that I can't do it, I chant inside my head.

"It's just that we're so busy with school." I rub the back of my neck. "You know."

"That's precisely why we need a break! Feel the wind under our wings, so to speak," Ray says.

"All vampires should stick together," Shannon adds.

I give them both a tight smile. "Just email me the details."

"We'll be glad to see you there!" Shannon chirps.

That makes one of us.

SIX

OWEN

I can feel Clay growing colder toward me, and for a blue-skinned vampire, that's saying a lot. We're in Monster Anatomy 101, and the professor has dismissed us. The sounds of my peers zipping up their bags surrounds me in the front row, but I don't jump on cleaning up just yet. To my left, my lab partner is hastily packing away his gear.

It's the third week of the semester, and with each lecture Clay has grown less and less talky and touchy. I suppose getting his wires crossed and exposing his dick to me in bed would do that.

Did I beat off to the memory of his abs, fangs, and cock? Well...that's irrelevant.

I need to apologize for making things weird. I reread my texts, and I can see why he'd think something different than what I meant.

"Hey, can we talk?"

"Hm," Clay says, without making eye contact.

I gulp, feeling the icy sting of his response. I look around and notice no one is within earshot. "Clay, you should know..."

He finally looks at me, those gorgeous purple eyes with a

hint of red, reaching into my soul. I'm not sure if vampire hypnotism is a thing, or if it's a fabricated legend. But being dick-matized—gay guys being enthralled by hot men—is so real. And Clay, the beautiful airhead, checks off all my boxes.

He's also a star athlete. Been there, done that, not willing to burn myself at the stake again.

I clear my throat. "There's a quiz next week."

"Oh?" He takes on that adorably confused expression that I've spotted on him during lecture. This time, however, it's warranted—*What kind of apology was that?*

"Uh, thanks, I guess?"

"I mean to say…" I shift up my glasses, then play with my notebook in front of me. "I know nothing about water polo."

"Eh? The quiz is on water polo?" He looks down and bites his lip. "I didn't realize that was part of anatomy class," he mutters with genuine, himbo sincerity.

I huff. "No, I mean you're a water polo player."

"Ah." He smiles. "So I'll do good on the quiz, eh?"

I shake my head. "No, forget the quiz. Well, don't, because it's a quarter of our grade…just listen!" I look around and notice almost everyone has left the classroom. "I'm sorry if I led you to believe something was happening between us. It wasn't my intention to come on to you. The truth is, I don't date water polo players. More importantly, we're lab partners, so we need to get along for this class."

He frowns and stands up, hiking his bag. "I get it. You made that very clear the other night."

The disappointment dripping from his tone hurts my soul. "I mean, come on," I murmur, pulling up my own bag. "You don't wanna hook up with me. All I do is talk academia, ask a mountain of questions, and spend my free time going to the museum for leisure. I certainly wouldn't be any fun in or out of bed."

I chuckle out of nervousness as I all but chase him out of the room. "And more importantly, I'll do as much of the work as I can and give you plenty of credit. I'll be interviewing my dryad friend...well his boyfriend is my friend."

Clay barely slows down as I ramble. "And you'll get half the credit. We can forget about any bedroom mishaps! And while I stick to my books, you'll have more time polo-ing in the water."

He finally stops, and I nearly bump into him. He turns around and levels with me. His cheekbones and perfect hair make him look like he belongs in a superhero comic book. How can someone be this handsome and even consider sticking his dick anywhere near the likes of me?

"Is that really all I am to you?" he asks with a flat tone.

I fidget with my backpack straps in the hallway. "I mean, you spend time at practice, and I basically live in the library," I say in a lower voice. Monsters mull about, paying us no mind in the hallway. "It would make life easier for both of us to stick to what we're doing."

He stares at me for a beat, then shrugs and looks away. "If that will make you the most comfortable."

"Thank you, Clay. We'll link up for another project session soon. Preferably with clothes on." I laugh nervously, point finger guns, and step back, but he simply nods.

"Okay. But Owen?"

I catch his gaze and he looks so serious as he steps backward. "You get to decide whom you want to hook up with, and so do I." With a wave, this gorgeous vampire turns and strolls away.

I'm left there stunned in the hallway. Among other surprises today, Clay used the word "whom" correctly.

"AND SO, HOW DO YOU EAT?"

I lean forward on my table in the dining hall, pen in hand, ready for the answer.

"With my mouth? With a fork?" Kovi sips more Ghosta Cola from his straw and giggles while his boyfriend bumps into his shoulder, quietly cracking up.

I huff. "I meant in your tree form?"

"Uh, I don't?" Tanner can barely contain his laughter at Kovi's answer.

"So, you don't like, dip your roots into a pasta sauce or anything?" I try to focus on my paper while the lovebirds continue to titter.

"Dude, have you met a plant before?" Kovi asks. The pair bursts into laughter like a couple of hyena shifters. If this is what love is like, remove me from the waiting list.

Then they gaze at each other with undeniable fondness. And when I look around, I notice the red banners on each table, along with more couples sitting closely.

It's Valentine's Day; my perpetually single ass forgot.

I dramatically close my book, and the couple doesn't even flinch. "Well, thank you for the information," I say in a deadpan tone.

"We're done already, Owen?" Kovi looks me up and down while Tanner holds him by the waist.

"I'm, um, all set," I lie. "I need to interview other species, to be honest."

"Are you sure we can't help you more? You haven't even asked about my branches." Kovi, to his credit, seems genuinely perplexed.

Tanner meanwhile, leans into his neck. "And all the things they can do," he purrs.

Kovi giggles, and I roll my eyes. "It's fine. Go enjoy Valentine's Day, you two." I stand up. "I'm sure the Student Union is having a dance or something," I say dolefully.

"That sounds fun!" Tanner remarks, gazing into his handsome boyfriend's eyes.

The couple chuckles again, and Kovi says, "Later, Owen," and then kisses Tanner.

I huff and stride for the exit. I'm happy for my closest human male friend considering all the drama that occurred last semester—and their whole lives—but that was rough.

Walking outside, I breathe in the icy sensations of the February air. My friends reminded me of how lonely I am, so maybe taking the bus to the museum will cheer me up. It's three weeks into the semester and I still haven't hooked up with a monster. Sure, I got to see Clay's hot ass, but I'm not interested in a surface-level connection with a dude I have nothing in common with.

Valentine's Day is reminding me that I want someone who wants to talk to me, listen to me, and be intimate with me. Which is a lot to ask since I'm a grumpy old nerd trapped in a twenty-one-year-old body.

I make the five-minute trek to the off-campus bus stop. The sight makes me almost want to gag; not only is the bus cubicle advertising Valentine's Day, but two harpies are making out on the bench. Feathers are flying as their wings retract and fan out repeatedly.

Okay, that's enough, I'm out. The museum will be there in a week.

I turn and grumble, "Friggin' hormones."

I power-walk away, past the Lin River. I stroll near the far side of the woods where students never congregate. Despite the

43

cold air, the long way back to my dorm sounds ideal. Street-lights guide my way through the night, and other than the occasional jogger, I'm alone.

I can tell this area doesn't get cleaned nearly as often as it should. This is further evidenced by an old, rusty birdhouse jutting from one of the poles with a sticker on it that reads, "Creelin Cockatoos."

"Ugh." I don't need to be reminded of my chaotic, sexy lab partner. So, I do what teenage boys did in high school when faced with a metal structure two feet above me— I take two quick steps and leap up. Then, my hand reaches up and I smack the sticker-faced birdhouse.

CLANG.

"Oh shit!" I swear just as the metal birdhouse falls. It turns out no one has reinforced the damn thing in decades. Fortu-nately, there are no witnesses around; I don't want to be caught defacing Creelin metro area property.

Before I can properly dash away, I hear a squeaking sound. *What is that?*

I crouch down closer to the now-grounded, tipped-over birdhouse. The riverside area is quiet, and the squeak arises again.

Is that...mewling?

Using my phone as a flashlight, I peer inside the birdhouse. I illuminate the source of the noise and it's...dark and hairy?

I gasp and step back, startled by the unknown. When it mewls again, I lean forward and scrutinize the inside of the house. The thing inside isn't a bird: it's hairy, twitching, and...

It's a bat! Apparently, a tiny bat has made this ancient bird-house his home.

"*Squeak!*"

I crouch closer to get a better look. When I shine the light on it again, it winces.

Holy shit—it's bleeding.

"Fuck..." I mutter. The poor thing has an injured wing. I'm no animal expert—some monsters can commune with animals, or so I've read—but even I know bats aren't supposed to bleed like that. And considering how bright the blood around it is, I'd say it's a fresh wound.

Shit, I did this?

"*Squeak*." It looks so tired, like it could die at any moment.

"No," I whisper gravely. I stand up and look around, as if the bat ambulance will arrive. But no, it's a dark evening, and I'm on my own. My breathing speeds up and I put my palms on my forehead. The waves of anxiety threaten to drown me; I haven't had a panic attack in years. But now the guilt is gnawing at my chest.

Before I can collapse, I attempt to visualize the air going in and out of my lungs. My pulse pounds, so I fixate on anything I can see. The river reflects the streetlights like an orange parade of manta rays. *Focus on the pretty colors...*

This gets my breathing to finally slow down. I shake out my wrists, knowing the panic attack is suppressed, for now.

"*Squeak*."

"It's okay, it's okay," I chant, half to myself, half to the animal who can't understand me. I peer at it again. "I'm going to...help you."

It mewls one last time before I dash away. Tears threaten to flood my eyes, but I refuse to cry. Not out of misplaced manliness, but out of determination—I am going to help this poor defenseless creature of the night.

THIRTY MINUTES LATER, I've returned with a backpack. I'm huffing as I crouch down since I ran all the way to campus and back. No one's around, which is both good and bad—I'd love someone, anyone more experienced to help, but I don't want any rogue creatures trying to eat it or anything. He deserves a shot at a normal bat life, the life I've almost taken away.

"Please say you're still okay," I mutter as I unzip my bag.

He mewls, and I swear he's being sarcastic, saying, "I can't go anywhere, asshat," or something to that effect.

"I'll...take care of you. I think." I bite my lip and put on my thick winter gloves. Slowly, I dab his wing with a towel, soaking the blood. Then, as gently as possible, I ease it into the tiny shoebox I've brought with me. Despite my haste, I remembered to poke air holes, tape the top so it acts as a hatch, and line it with more paper towels. This little buddy should be comfortable in the tiny makeshift bed I've made for him.

Well, I mean, as comfortable as one can be after having their wing severely injured by some terrible human.

"Let's get you out of here." I close the lid, catch my breath, and then swiftly stride back to campus.

My mind buzzes with questions. Am I allowed to have it back on campus? Will my roommate be okay with it? Most importantly, what can I do to make the little buddy okay again? He needs to take flight and be free.

I'm supposed to be a doctor-in-training. Some healer I am, I can't even take care of an injured bat. *What if he ends up...?*

The very thought of him not making it sends a wave of anxiety through my bones, and I clutch the shoebox harder. My eyes prickle with the thought of death, even of an animal. I feel so guilty, and in that guilt, I've bonded with the little guy. I can't go back to my room. *But maybe...*

I don't even think. My feet are on autopilot, zooming me

through the quad, as I try to brainstorm for any deep-seated knowledge about nocturnal animal life.

I'm not myself when I knock on the door with a shaky hand. That familiar burn of a panic attack crawls up my spine, and I once again try to focus on my breathing. Air in my lungs, my feet on the ground, I'm safe....

When the door opens, it's like the panic attack evaporates. The face in front of me makes my heart skip a beat and my brain restart. A kindling of hope glows in my chest.

I don't even let the dude say a word.

"I didn't know where else to go," I say in a pathetic whine.

Clay stares at me, his eyebrows scrunching together. "Owen?"

SEVEN

CLAY

Owen Bhat is standing in my doorway, clutching a shoebox in his shaking hands, biting his lip. His forehead wrinkles, and his eyes are red and watery. He nods repeatedly, and he licks his lip with cautious hope. "Please," he whispers under his breath.

I scratch at my temple. "You didn't know where else to go?" I repeat.

Owen shakes his head, holding his breath. His nutmeg-vanilla scent washes over me.

I drink in the sight of my lab partner—disheveled hair, smudged glasses, large winter coat, chapped lips. *Adorable.* Absolutely adorable.

He makes my chest flutter, just at the sight of him. My throat thickens, and I'm suddenly very thirsty. In more ways than one.

Stop being a horny bastard. He needs help.

"I thought you didn't want to talk to me," I say, and I sound resentful even to my own ears. We've gone too long with barely speaking, and now he's here with some sort of shoe emergency.

I should be able to help with that, though. I mean, Bran went Speedo shopping with Steve. I'm sure I can help Owen find a footwear solution. I don't think we're the same size, but maybe he can borrow something of Yuki's.

"Please, Clay? Can you just see if you can do something to help him?"

Blinking, I peer behind Owen. Maybe he has a friend with a problem? While a few dorm-room doors are open, and music and conversation are spilling out, there's no one nearby. I tried to go out tonight, but begged off early. V-Day means too many sappy couples in love.

I show him my palms and shrug. "Come on in." I step back, giving him space to enter my dorm.

Shutting the door behind him, Owen starts pacing, still grasping the box. "He's hurt, and I'm worried about him, and I'm pre-med so I'm supposed to know what to do but I don't, I just don't."

My head shakes slightly, and I hold up a hand. "*Who's* hurt? Your Clawverse hightops?"

Owen's eyes narrow. "What? No. The bat." He shoves the shoebox toward me, and I accept it automatically.

"What bat?" The box has holes punched into it. It's good that I recognized that, otherwise I would've shaken the box like a present.

"Be careful when you take off the lid. I hope he's okay."

What on Earth is going on here? What kind of bat did he find?

I set the box on my bed and carefully open it. Inside is the smallest bit of black fuzz with big eyes and fangs, along with black membranous wings. The fuzz mewls at us, and there's some fresh blood on his wing. Poor little guy. "You found a vampire bat?"

Owen tugs at his hair. "Is it a vampire bat? I wasn't sure."

I nod as I gently slide a finger in the box to pet his head. He makes a squeaking noise.

"He's hurt. I knocked something over, and it damaged his wing." Owen sits down next to me on the bed, then gets up again, then sits down.

Instantly, I'm on high alert. "Then we need to get him to a veterinarian."

Owen pauses at me and blinks. "A vet? Why...didn't I think of that?"

I can't help but grin. "I have my moments."

"I don't have money to pay for a vet," Owen admits.

"I do. Don't worry about it. Let's go." I have a scholarship I don't need since I've had twenty years to gather money. Other than a few early years when I was testing the limits of vampire life, I haven't spent much of it.

"You'll go with me?"

"Definitely," I say, flashing my fangs and hopefully giving him a reassuring smile, although we need to get a move on if he has serious injuries. "Back you go into the dark, buddy," I coo at the bat as I put the lid back on. "Just let me get my shoes."

"Thank you so much," Owen breathes. "I was so worried about him."

I put a hand on his shoulder and then remove it quickly. "Let's get him some help."

Fifteen minutes later, we're pulling up to the Creelin Veterinary Urgent Care. I drove, and Owen called ahead of time to get us on the list. I made sure to remember my wallet and keys this time, but I forgot my phone.

The waiting room is large, new, and pristine, with industrial flooring and cleaning supplies at the ready. There's an older man sitting in the back holding a dachshund, and a pair of women playing on their phones with a parrot in a cage on the floor near them. The walls are covered with framed photographs of the pets they've taken care of, from cats and dogs to snakes and frogs to fire lizards and wolves.

The vampire behind the counter looks up as we walk in. "We're the ones who called a few minutes ago," I say. "We've got an injured vampire bat."

I notice a sign on the wall that reads, *We triage your pet's emergency based on the following criteria: Critical: broken bones, poisoning, excessive bleeding; Urgent: Constipation, sneezing, vomiting; Stable: Fleas, broken nails, abscesses.* With my nail, I tap on *Critical.* "This is us."

She nods. "Are you in our system?"

"No."

"Then why don't you complete this paperwork after you bring him to the back?" she asks. Thank the monster god the veterinarians aren't hung up on bureaucracy.

Following Owen, I take the clipboard and go with her into an exam room where I fill out the forms. After I hand them to a tech, we wait and wait and wait.

"I bet this isn't how you wanted your Valentine's Day to go?" Owen asks in a facetious tone. I can tell he's fighting exhaustion, anxiety, and guilt.

Except...my day perked up the moment Owen knocked on my door. "I'm good with it," I tell him.

Owen opens his mouth to say something else when the veterinarian quietly comes in. "I'm Dr. Soto, and I'm happy to help." She's a human and is clearly used to not spooking animals or monsters. "Let's see your little bat," she says, placing the box on a towel on the exam table. She gently opens the box lid. "Aww, friend. What happened to you?"

"I accidentally hurt him," Owen says. "I didn't know he was

in this old birdhouse, and I knocked it over. I didn't mean to injure him. I feel terrible."

I sling an arm around Owen's shoulders. "No one thinks you'd hurt anyone on purpose, let alone an innocent creature."

"It's good that you got him to help quickly," Dr. Soto says.

She carefully does some assessment of his vital signs, respiratory system, and alertness, then turns to us. "I'm going to dress his wound and give you some medicine for him. But after he is healed, he's still going to need rehabilitation. We could take him inpatient, but with it being Valentine's Day, we're short-staffed. So we'll have to call around and see who has space for twenty-four-hour care of a vampire bat. But he does need to go to a rescue facility."

Owen wrinkles his brow and bites his lip. "How expensive is it?

"Don't worry about it," I mutter.

"I do worry about it. I can't afford it."

"Can we just rehabilitate him?" I ask the veterinarian. "What do we have to do?"

Dr. Soto tilts her head back and forth. "Bats make poor pets because they're wild animals and nocturnal."

I show her my fangs. "I'm wild and nocturnal too."

Owen must be feeling a little better because he playfully shoves me with his shoulder.

"Well, it's not entirely unheard of to have a vampire nurse a vampire bat, and we do have handouts on their care," she says, thumbing through some flyers in cubbies on the wall. "Let me get you a few. If you're interested in taking on the responsibility, we can support you with that. He will need to have regular checkups, and call us immediately if his symptoms worsen. He's going to need care, and then a lot of space for flying."

What else am I going to do with my time? I've been spending the past few weeks rehabbing my bruised ego from

Owen's rejection. I'm not sure why it got to me so much, but it's kept me from any hookups.

And the idea of being able to spend more time with him is definitely enticing.

I look over at Owen. "Bat dads?"

He nods. "Bat dads."

I hold out my knuckles, and he fist-bumps me.

After receiving more instructions from the veterinarian and paying the bill—Owen sees the amount, and I have to whisper in his ear that it's no big deal—we head back out to the car.

Next stop is the twenty-four-hour FangMart superstore. There, as Owen cuddles the shoebox, we pick out supplies.

"I'll be expecting you to respond to my texts regarding the updated care of Bat Nathanson."

A snicker escapes my lips. "Bat Nathanson?"

Owen turns a shade darker, like he's embarrassed, as he looks away. "Well yeah." He shifts up his glasses in the cutest way. "The doctor said he was a boy. We have to name him. The best Matt I know is that indie alternative singer dude from the turn of the millennium."

My heart swells. "You know Matt Nathanson?"

His eyes fill with surprise. "*You* know Matt Nathanson?"

A laugh bubbles from my chest as I cradle the shoebox. "Dude, Matt Nathanson is my jam. I was in my twenties twenty years ago, remember?"

"Oh right...the vampire age thing." His coldness seems cute, like an afterthought or accessory.

I smile at the little guy in my arms. "Hear that? Your papa wants to call you Bat Nathanson."

Owen stares at me skeptically. "Papa?" I gaze at my lab partner and take in his adorable face. He sighs and rolls his eyes. "Fine. If I'm his Papa, I guess that makes you his bat Daddy."

I snicker. "Well, then—"

"No, I am not calling you Daddy," he says with a frown. With that, we both start cracking up. I didn't expect to take in a pet on Valentine's Day, but with this new connection to Owen, I'm not complaining.

CHAPTER

EIGHT

OWEN

We own a terrarium together. Or, more accurately, we're nursing a bat together, and that involved buying a terrarium. We also bought woodchips, newspapers, hypoallergenic paper towels, and bottles. We went ahead and threw in some toys when checking out of the pet store.

And by "we," I mean Clay. With the paltry school allowance my parents give me every month, I can barely afford my bus pass to go to the museum. I can't get mad at them—they're hard-working immigrants paying to get me through school. I don't have time for a job, so I can't simply buy out pet stores at the drop of a witch's hat. But Clay is apparently well off; he spends money like it's not a big deal, and I'm not sure if it's all the stipend from the Organization of Monster Enhancement— we all call them the homies at the OME—or from like, a water polo scholarship, or whatever.

That voice in my head that resents jocks for getting everything is still there, but it's quieter now because Clay has really shown up for this little animal.

For almost two weeks, I've gone to Clay's dorm in the

evening to visit our bat. And each time, Clay has been a superb fur parent. Maybe it's a vampire kindred spirit thing, but regardless of the reason, he's been nothing but caring. He changes the lining, makes sure the blanket covers him during the day to keep his little box dark, and changes the bandages just the way the vet told us to.

This jock has shown me his nurturing side, and his competence is attractive AF...I mean admirable. Admirable AF.

I knock on his dorm door as usual and I hear him say "Come in!"

I walk in and smile. "Hey!" I turn to my left. "Hey, Yuki."

His roommate gives me a fake smile, then quickly packs up his things. Before I can tell him he doesn't need to leave, he dashes off. Does he also have vampire speed? He's been generally accommodating to me and our bat, but I haven't gotten to know him. I don't even know if he's a monster or not.

Clay is sitting on his bed, slowly unraveling the dressing from the bat's wing as it lies down on a towel on his lap. I take a seat next to them. "How's he doing?"

"Bat Nathanson is a trooper. Check it out." Clay removes the last bandage. I notice he's using gloves as instructed and I try to ignore the fact that our thighs are touching. He smells damn good, too. *Focus, Owen.*

"How's the wound?"

"All but gone." Clay gently lifts him up to me. "Just like the doc said it would be."

"Aw, he's healed now."

"Yup. Our baby is almost ready to leave the nest."

My head goes dizzy with a rush of emotions. The idea of us being co-parents is a little too thrilling, and the thought of this ending is a little too disappointing. Why should I care? I want the bat to get better, and I want my friend—no, lab partner—

and me to pass the class. Then life will go back to the way it was before.

I shake my head and open my backpack. "I have the notes from class."

"Oh, sweet, thanks." He puts our pet back in the terrarium and shuts the glass door.

"You can copy them." I take a pair of gloves from his desk which now exclusively houses bat things—I hope we don't get in trouble with the staff. "Meanwhile, I'll take a turn feeding BN."

"Blood bottle is in the fridge," he says. He picks up the notes and scrutinizes my work while I open the terrarium. We spend the next several minutes quietly doing our respective tasks. He asks questions about what he missed in lecture while I coddle the bat. The fuzzy thing slurps the red liquid from the bottle, and if I didn't know any better, I'd say he was smiling. The fact that he's almost healed makes my heart flutter.

Or maybe it's the fact that Clay and I are so damn domestic. And each day I like it more. Visions of us doing this for years flood my brain, but I tamp those down. I'm going to be a doctor for monsters, and Clay is going to slowly age and stay hot and make some other dude happy. What we're doing now is not what either of us signed up for.

After an hour, I place the bat back in the glass box. Clay paid for the tower for our pet to hang from, and later leap off of. So, since his wing is now sans-dressing, I place him on the hanging piece of wood. He stands on it for a moment, then falls over, so I catch him. "Woah, there."

I do it two more times, then frown. "Damn," I say.

"What?" Clay is now crouching next to me.

"Poor thing." I glance to my left and see Clay staring in concern. His beautiful face is lit up by the orange light of the desk lamp. His high cheekbones, perfectly combed wavy hair, and chiseled jawline are not interesting to me—there's no way I want to lean in and bridge the three centimeters between his mouth and mine.

"What's wrong?" Clay asks.

"Bat Nathanson won't fly." I place him on the hanging piece, and after two seconds, he falls over. "The doctor said once we remove the dressing, the little guy would happily flap around."

"Oh no." The two of us watch as the bat once again prefers the tiny towel bed we've made for him. Everyone knows bats should prefer to sleep upside down.

"Maybe we should call the doctor again," Clay suggests.

"She'll just give us the same information and then charge us a copay," I grumble. I bite my lip and remove my gloves. Clay does the same, and we sanitize our hands. His arms bulge fantastically through his black T-shirt, and I lick my lips.

Of course! "I've got an idea!" I grin at Clay.

"What?"

"We could do bat rehabilitation. It's so obvious."

"Huh?"

"He's a vampire bat, and you're a vampire!" I snap my fingers. "It's perfect. You can teach him how to fly!"

"Wha....what?" Clay looks distressed but I look down at the terrarium.

"Think about it!" I point at the bat in the glass, and he wakes up. Clay leans in, and I notice his pretty face in the reflection. "You can show Bat Nathanson how to fly! Take him almost literally under your wing! It's perfect!"

"Squeak!" Bat Nathanson smiles at us; if I didn't know any better, I'd say he understands us.

"See? Even he thinks it's a good idea!"

"I, uh..." Clay swallows. "I...I don't...fly," he mutters.

We both stand up. "Not fly, glide." I wave my hand in front of him. "You know what I mean, take to the skies."

I whip out my phone and pace around. "My friend Tanner knows the best places in the West Woods."

"Owen."

"And of course, I'll be there the whole time. We can even learn about anatomy while you fly around: two bats, one stone! Ha!"

"Owen."

I keep clicking on my phone. "So, when are you free? I know you have polo practice, and you'll probably be tired after. How about a day that you're off? The weather is supposed to be nice next week."

"Owen, I CAN'T FLY!"

I pause at his outburst. Clay looks truly distraught, his sorrowful eyes beginning to glisten.

"What?"

He huffs and his shoulders sag. "I...I have never flown...or glided. I can't fly," he admits, voice laced with despondence.

My eyebrows furrow. "But...you're..."

"A vampire?" he murmurs with a frown.

I swallow. "No, old. You've been at this for decades."

He grumbles and lies on his bed, turning away. I glance at our pet, who seems to frown in the terrarium. The bat's eyes say, "Go console him," so I do.

"Hey," I say, sitting next to him.

"I'm a forty-year-old loser who can't fly," he says quietly. He crosses his arms and his lips tremble.

The need to comfort Clay burns so brightly in my heart, I can't deny it. I rub his back up and down. "Dude, it'll be okay."

"No, it won't," he replies in a soft tone. "I've tried to teach myself for years."

I never thought a sexy guy like him would have anything to

be so self-conscious about. "Clay, I don't think any less of you just because you technically haven't flown yet."

"You don't?" He turns to me on the bed.

"No," I reply with a smile.

"Don't you think I'm just a stupid jock?"

I snigger. "I never said stupid. You're an athlete, but also a caring guy."

He gazes at me, hope blooming in his purple eyes. The strangest spark of something else darts between the two of us.

"This changes nothing."

"What?" he asks.

"Clay, we need to teach Bat Nathanson how to fly." I point to the terrarium, and our pet squeaks in response.

Clay sits up, and I reluctantly remove my hand from his— chiseled, muscular—back. "But, Owen, I don't—"

"And we can teach you how to fly, too." I stand with renewed energy. "It's perfect!"

"Huh?"

"You can both learn how to fly together. A vampire and a vampire bat!" I clap my hands. "Anthropologically, this is the coolest thing I've ever been a part of! I can take notes and use different colored ink for each of you!"

I rub my palms together, but Clay stares at me like I'm speaking Portuguese. "But...you..." He huffs and asks, "You don't think I'm a loser because I can't fly?"

"Heck no," I reply, hiking up my backpack.

"I thought you detested me."

I snicker. "I didn't appreciate you flashing your body to me a week after we met, but I respect your hard work." I shrug. "It's nothing to be ashamed of, but of course, I won't tell anyone about you learning how to fly."

Clay looks down and bites his lip in the most adorable way.

I can almost see the gears turning in his himbo brain—no, not himbo brain, handsome brain.

Before I can leave, I'm overcome with a sudden force wrapped around me. "Oof!"

Clay...is hugging me?

"Thank you. For not telling anyone," he whispers.

My eyebrows might not ever go down. I pat his shoulder and absorb his scent for a brief moment. "Mmm...no...problem."

He backs away, and I make a hasty exit. "Text you later for our next, um...study session," I say.

"Peace," he says, and the bat squeaks as I gently close the door.

My mind spins while I power-walk down the corridor, a difficult feat considering the massive hard-on that threatens my jeans right now. Something has shifted between Clay and me, and for the first time in my life, I'm going with the flow.

Because I want to help the two vampires in my life learn how to fly. That's *definitely* the only reason my heart is spinning in my chest and I have a goofy grin on my lips.

NINE

CLAY

It's a windy early-March night with no clouds and a bright moon, so Owen decreed that the conditions were perfect for flight lessons. Glide lessons. Whatever.

We're in the forest at the edge of the school by the Cree River. A few students are walking to the dorms and some zombies are taking out the trash and preparing the campus for tomorrow, but for the most part we're alone, thank the monster god. I don't want those students from the Vampire Gliding Club to find me.

Since Owen doesn't fly, I have no idea how he knows the correct method to teach me, but given that he's read just about every book in the library, I'm trusting him. After all, he's smarter than me. Although it does feel like I'm being instructed on how to have sex by a virgin who read about it in a textbook.

Is he a virgin? Is that why he ran away from me so long ago?

I glance down at him. Owen's curly hair moves in the wind, and his glasses slip down his nose.

I don't think so. Maybe he's just shy. I want to ask, but I'm standing in a tree, and circumstances aren't ideal.

Pay attention, Clay.

As I use the rubber soles of my running shoes to grip a sturdy pine tree branch ten feet off the ground, my movement causes a clump of needles to fall off. I watch them spiral down. *Nrgh.* That's what's going to happen to me.

"I believe I'm still subject to gravity," I yell into the heavy breeze. "And it will hurt when I face-plant on the earth."

Owen's got Bat Nathanson in a roomy carrier at his feet, and they're downhill a ways. I guess he figures that I should go first before we let the bat out. "You're not going to face-plant. You'll catch the gale."

"Maybe." I can't keep the skepticism out of my voice. "I just don't feel like I'm aerodynamic."

He cups his hands around his mouth. "Planes fly. So do birds. And vampires. All you need to do is practice."

I scrub my face with my free hand.

I don't know why I'm doing this. Even with my monster speed-healing, I'm still going to be covered in bruises. And it's not going to work. I've never been able to do it. I feel heavy, both in body and spirit.

"Let's get this over with," I mutter under my breath.

"First, close your eyes," Owen calls.

"Not sure that will help. I need to see where I'm going," I call back.

"But right now you need to feel the wind beneath your wings. So to speak."

I snort, the wind making the tree branch sway. "Aren't you too young for that song?"

"What song?"

That makes me shake my head and feel my age. "'Wind Beneath My Wings' by Bette Midler. My mom used to sing it when I was a kid."

Mom.

My chest aches, as it always does when I think of her and Dad.

Then I suck my cheeks in, remembering the last things she said to me before they kicked me out after I turned.

You're dangerous, and the Halloween Wave ruined your life. You'll never amount to anything. We don't want to see you ever again. Leave.

Now, with the space of two decades, I know they were just scared I was going to bite and turn them, but back then, her words were brutal. To be fair, I was pretty damn thirsty when I first turned, but they've remained firmly anti-monster, so I've stayed out of their lives. They have a perfect, white-picket-fence house out in California. While I've literally *seen* them in the past two decades—from afar—I haven't spoken with them since then.

I shake my head to clear the bad memories.

A particularly strong blast of wind hits me from the back.

"You'll have to play me that song," Owen says. "For now, when the next blast comes, jump into it."

Might as well get this over with.

I close my eyes and wait until a forceful wind gust almost pushes me off the branch, so I spread my arms wide and let it.

And I fall to the ground, my chin hitting a rock and pain slicing through me. "Oof." *Ow.* Dammit.

I *knew* that was going to happen.

Footsteps sound near me. "Clay! Are you okay?"

Knifing myself into a sitting position, I dust off my knees. "Yeah, I'm fine."

"You kind of fell like a stone."

"Well, I told you so."

Owen's wringing his hands. "I'm so sorry, I might need to do some more reading on this. I thought it was just a matter of catching the air currents. Maybe we need to get you a mattress or something that we can use to soften your fall."

"Or we could just go to the gym and try it on the mats," I say. Depending on how busy it is, it could be less public, too.

He tilts his head. "Do you think we can catch enough of a breeze indoors?"

"Probably not."

"Mm...but we could work on your form." He purses his lips. "Maybe I should rethink this. I'm not really into...gym culture."

"Why not?"

"No reason. I just want to make sure you're one with the wind, that's all."

Okay, he said that way too hastily. What's Owen got against gyms? Or maybe it's the people in the gyms?

"Do you want to see if Bat Nathanson wants to try it tonight?"

Owen gives me a grateful smile at the change of subject. "Sure." He lets BN out of the carrier. "Come on, little buddy," he coos. "You can do it."

Flapping his wings a few times, BN tries to fly but falls flat to the carrier. At least I don't feel so alone.

Owen scoops him up, and coaxes him inside the carrier. "You can try again later, Bat Nathanson."

"You can do it," I agree, trying to give BN enthusiasm I don't feel for myself. "Next time."

"I like caring for him." Owen's tone is thoughtful. "I'm sure he'll figure it out."

I glance around at the mostly empty part of campus. "Should we try flight lessons another night?"

"Or do you want to try the gym now? I think the evenings are free for the use of students."

"Fine," I say. "If anything, it'll be better to fall on a mat rather than the ground."

We walk across campus. I'm holding BN's carrier in one hand, and my other hand is free. If only Owen would take it, but he doesn't.

The gym is brightly lit, and a few of the baseball team is leaving as we head inside. But when I check in at the front desk and walk into the open-plan room, I freeze. Owen almost stumbles into my back.

"What is it?" Owen asks.

I shake my head. "This won't work."

"Why not?"

Might as well tell him the truth. "The entire Vampire Gliding Enthusiasts Club is over at the climbing wall."

"Who are the—"

Spinning on my heel, I walk right out again.

Owen picks up Bat Nathanson's carrier and follows behind me, calling, "Seriously, Clay, who was that?"

"There's a group of vampires who love gliding, and they've asked me repeatedly to join their club. But since, as you know, I can't do it..." I throw up my hands.

Owen studies my face, sincerity written all over him. "Clay, I'd never embarrass you in front of your peers. All I'm trying to do is help you figure this out. I think you *can* fly. Just no one's taught you yet."

"I hate feeling insecure," I mutter.

He tips his head to the side. "You?"

I frown. "Yes, I feel insecure sometimes. I hate admitting that, too, but I'm older and not smart and can't fly..."

A smile spreads across Owen's face. "I like all those things about you."

"That I'm not smart and can't fly?" I bark out a laugh.

"No. That you're real. You're pretty perfect looking, and having some things not be perfect for you—" he shrugs—"I guess it makes you seem more relatable. Less intimidating."

"Thanks, I think."

Although the fact that Owen likes me warms my cold heart just a bit.

A FEW DAYS LATER, Owen and I are walking with BN between us, headed to find another place to practice gliding, when we pass Professor Robinson.

"Hey, Professor," I call.

"Octavia," she corrects.

"I have trouble with addressing you that way," Owen admits. "I can appreciate using the name you prefer, but it feels like it's less respectful."

"Do you respect me?" she asks point blank.

"Of course," he says.

"Then, no problem here." She peers into the carrier. "What do you boys have in this box?"

"That's Bat Nathanson," I say, and put it on the ground so we can open it up. I pull BN out, who clings to the underside of my hand.

Octavia leans forward, tilting her head to scrutinize BN.

"Well, well, well," she says. "If you don't have a familiar."

"A familiar?" Owen asks.

"An animal who understands and obeys only you," Octavia clarifies.

"Like a pet?" I ask. "I've heard of familiars, but I thought they were something different."

"Not quite like a pet. It seems he might be bonded to you both. It's unusual for that to happen but not unheard of. The way he's clinging to both of you, it's so obvious his familiar bond is strong with you as a pair." She tries to hold BN, who wiggles with discomfort until Owen takes him back. She gives us both a knowing smile. "It's a good thing he's a familiar because pets aren't allowed on campus. How delightful you found him! Oh, monster science in action, I highly approve. Keep up the good work, and see you in class."

We both stare at her back as she walks away.

"Do you think she meant that?" Owen asks. "That BN is bonded to both of us?"

I tickle the little guy under his chin, and he nips at my finger affectionately. "It's possible. He doesn't seem in a hurry to get out of our care."

"I thought he was just taking time to recover." Owen rubs BN's head with his fingertip. If BN could purr, I bet he'd be doing it right now.

"I do think he needs time, but it seems more than that. I think he really likes being with us. So, maybe he is bonded." I smile, flashing my fangs. "That's super cool."

"Agreed." We put BN back in his carrier, and then start walking again.

"So, regarding where we should practice, all of these places feel so exposed," I admit. "Like I'm going to have public humiliation after public humiliation, when the point is to avoid that."

"Then maybe we need to go somewhere far from campus. Stokerbram Park has all those gorges, perfect for catching breezes. Too bad it's not close by."

"That's a drive, though," I muse. "It might be better to stay there overnight. Otherwise, it's a very long day."

"I...didn't mean to suggest that you...that we...go."

I smirk. "It's a great idea. Just one little getaway for you, me, and the baby bat."

Do I mind spending a weekend with Owen?

Absolutely not.

Am I looking for an excuse to get him into a hotel room by himself?

Absolutely.

Owen gulps. "It could be a good idea, but I don't have a lot of room in my budget for travel."

I wave a hand. "Don't worry about the hotel. You're teaching me to fly. It's the least I can do, making sure you're comfortable and not too tired. And give you a mini vacation."

"Mm...I have been meaning to get away..." He seems to mull it over for a beat, then shrugs. "All right. Let's do it. A getaway for you, me, and Bat Nathanson." His face shines with excitement. He pushes up his glasses, and the gesture is so hot, I want to ask him to do it ten times over.

Don't make it weird, Clay.

"Yes, we should do it," I say, echoing his words. I quickly add, "Platonically. We'll...platonically do it."

Whatever that means.

TEN

OWEN

What was I thinking, suggesting a road trip with Clay? Sure, he's paying for the hotel, and we'll be in two separate queen beds. And yes, I'm invested in helping him learn to fly in a more natural environment. There will be plenty of ledges and scenic vistas for both him and BN to try to take flight. We can even take some time to work on our various projects for anatomy class.

Two college dudes platonically getting away and studying in a bedroom. Yeah, that's totally a thing that happens, right?

"Can I ask you a question?"

I turn to the driver's seat to take a good look at Clay. He's driving on the highway while I hold the terrarium in my lap, covered in a towel. The morning sunlight means our pet should be asleep, but sunshine gives Clay an almost ethereal glow. He's less pale, more warm in color, and the light makes his dark hair glisten. Between the high cheekbones and strong neck, in a profile view, he still looks like a statue sculpted by the monster god.

I'm glad I have to hold this box, otherwise my lap and any

motion in my pants might be exposed to the world. Or, at least, to Clay.

He looks at me expectantly then back out at the highway. "Owen?"

I shake my head. "Um, yeah?"

"I need you sharp if I'm gonna learn how to fly." He chuckles and grips the steering wheel with one hand. "Like I said, can I ask you a personal question?"

"Sure." I swallow. "We have time to kill. At least for another hour."

"Yeah. And I think getting to know you will help plant the seeds of trust for our partnership." He glances at me in alarm. "*Lab* partnership. And flying."

"Well, apparently we share a familiar." I grin and lift the towel just a smidge—our bat is still sleeping. "So I'm not opposed to some small talk."

Clay relaxes and stares out the windshield. "So, why do you hate jocks?"

Oh, it's that question. I clear my throat. "I don't...hate jocks."

"You could've fooled me," he replies.

The box in my lap is suddenly so interesting that I fixate on it. "I have a...sordid history with athletic boys."

"What, did they shove you into lockers as a kid?" He glances at me, and his look changes from humorous to concerned in a split second.

Trees zoom past us out the window. I sigh and say, "No. I mean, I dealt with the typical racial slurs in elementary school. Then homophobic jeers in middle school."

"Shit, really?"

"I'm an Indian kid going to school in America. Plus, the glasses, occasional panic attacks, being skinny, and later gay." I shrug and rub the toweled box. "I was never going to be high on the list of popularity."

"Shit, racial slurs, too? Kids are still doing that?"

"Unfortunately, colorism is a timeless phenom," I mutter. "But that cooled down a lot in high school."

"And jocks...bullied you?" His voice is laced with sympathy, and it makes me smile.

"Not even. The reason I don't date athletic boys is because I *did* date athletic boys."

"Huh?"

We lock eyes for a brief moment. "A dude in high school. Then two dudes at my previous university. Short-term relationships with guys who made being on teams their whole personality."

"Owen..."

I stare out the windshield. "It's not like they hid me or bullied me or anything. I got to lose my virginity, too, which, ya know, score!" I give a facetious laugh, but Clay gazes at me with a neutral face. "What they did was...well, not so good for my self-esteem."

"What did they do?" he asks quietly.

"Eventually they called me boring. Just because I liked reading, museums, and learning about monsters."

"Aw man," he replies.

My throat feels dry as I swallow. "I think maybe I talked a bit too much about my fascination with monsters. And maybe that alienated them because they were human. Even though I liked them, I wasn't enough for them."

"Hey—"

"It's for the best. They never exactly comforted me when I had anxiety."

"Owen—"

"I shouldn't have been blinded by the tight abs and nice biceps." I give another feeble laugh. "We didn't have a lot in common. But like, I was a horny seventeen-year-old.

What's a guy to do? You remember what that was like, right?"

Clay raises an eyebrow. "Not really, since I used to go to drive-in movie dates on the back of dinosaurs. Because according to you, I'm old AF."

A beat later, we're both cracking up, and I try not to jostle the terrarium. "I did *not* say that," I say through a chuckle.

"I mean, I am though." After we calm down, he gives me a serious look. "Owen, I'm sorry that happened to you."

"Ancient history. Coming to Creelin was my fresh start." I shrug. "Now I have monster friends. Like Kovi."

"And me!" He shoots me an over-the-top grin, and I snicker.

"Yes, I suppose teaching you how to fly makes us friends, Cannon."

"It does. And for the record, I don't think you need to change for anyone. You're a catch, and don't you forget it."

His simple words have a stranglehold on my heart. "Thanks," I murmur. With that, we stay friendly and quiet as the miles fly by on our road trip.

STOKERBRAM PARK IS GORGEOUS—GORGES?—ON this lovely March evening. Clay parks us in a lot near a trail specifically marked to lead us to the waterfalls. Like the gentleman he is, he takes our terrarium as we stroll a mile into the wooded park. His vampire strength is impressive, and even in his dark thermal shirt under a vest, his arms bulge fantastically.

Several minutes later, we stop by the running water. I make a small, blanketed area on a flat rock to place the terrarium. Then, I roll out Clay's extra-large sleeping bag to soften his landing. Lastly, I place my bag down and take out my notebook. It's so quiet, with nary a bird in the sky, save for the sound of the flowing water in the gorge. No one is around, so it's like we have all of nature to ourselves.

With our pet settled, I take a good look at the scene before me. "Woah," I say, breathlessly. I spend so much time in cities, being in nature is almost overwhelming. The evergreen trees are massive and tower over us. Before me, the waterfall is several meters high, and I can picture Clay leaping off and flying above the watery gorge toward our picnic area.

"All right, I'm ready!"

I look up to see Clay several feet in the air, standing on a branch. *Oh, we're just getting into it?* He waves at me with his black winter gloves. In his green beanie cap, he's adorable; it's so unfair this buff monster jock also has a cute face. I shift up my glasses and give him a thumbs-up.

"Feel the breeze?" I ask, hopefully loud enough for him to hear. Wait, of course he can hear me; he has superior senses.

He looks up, then back down at me and nods.

"So, remember, the air currents are your friend," I declare. "All of my research has led me to believe that vampires can adjust their density based on their willingness to fly."

He rubs his hands and nods, looking around.

"Just listen to the breeze and let it lift you!"

Clay takes a deep breath, and...

PLOP!

My eyes track him as he falls onto the sleeping bag. I wince in disappointment. His accelerated healing will assist him with any bruises, but his spiritual motivation might take a beating. I rush over and help him up even though he's strong enough to stand on his own. I only allow my hands to linger on his—very buff—arms through the black thermal for a moment before stepping back.

"Still no dice," he says while dusting off the shoulders of his puffer vest.

I frown. "Maybe your vest is weighing you down. Less weight means more lift, right?"

He unzips his vest. "Trying to get me naked, Bhat?"

I sputter and look away, feeling my cheeks heat. "I'm just... brainstorming here."

"Hm. All right." He puts away his vest and hat. Then, with superhuman agility, climbs up the tree. His vampire powers continue to fascinate me. And yes, seeing his strength in action with one less layer is all sorts of hot.

He can't possibly be into me after I continuously reject him. This getaway in a romantic forest is strictly for science.

Clay tries twice more and each time immediately falls flat. I tilt my head and sigh; I swore things would be different out here in nature.

"This is the worst," he grumbles. I feel for him, this sexy vampire who's quickly become my friend. The shame on his pretty face is undeniable, and I want to touch his face and take the pain away.

Pain. Hm. That gives me an idea.

"Clay...you...suck."

He stares at me like I just sprouted another head. "*Pardon?*"

"You're a vampire who can't glide." I raise my voice in an attempt to berate him further. "How will Bat Nathanson learn anything with *you* as his guide?"

"I'm...I'm *trying.*" His brow furrows. He seems genuinely offended, shaking out his hands and frowning at me.

"I bet you're not even a real jock. You clearly don't have the athleticism to float along the winds of the woods, a feat so simple a pigeon could do it."

He glares at me in shock. "I...I am. What...what are you...?"

"Then prove it," I say with a firmer tone. I get in his space, point at his muscly chest, and add, "Prove to me this all wasn't a waste of time. That I'm not better off spending my time with another vampire."

"Owen—"

"You claim to be this playboy athlete, then make like the wicked witch and take to the skies."

"But—"

"Do it." I put my finger on his chest and push him backward. "Show me you're not worthless, Cannon. Show me...show me you can *fucking* fly."

He growls and steps back, his face filled with rage and determination. "Fine," he grumbles, ripping off his gloves. In a blur, he climbs up the tree and stands on the biggest branch. He closes his eyes, presumably breathing in the forest air. All I can hear is the nearby waterfall.

Hopefully, my little one-man show worked.

After a beat, he rips off his shirt—holy monster god, the man is ripped. I don't even get to enjoy it because he shakes out his shoulders, steps back, and...

He leaps. For a long, glorious moment, he floats in the air. The sun streaks across his beautiful half-naked body.

Then, like a paper airplane, he glides down and crashes into the mud. Notably, however, he's not on the sleeping bag two feet in front of the tree.

He's a few yards away from me, so I scramble to help him up. "Agh," he groans, wiping his chest. I try not to stare at that pristine torso—pale bluish skin, tight abs, and a flat chest—as he wipes off dirt.

"Clay!"

"I know, I know," he grumbles, prying a twig from out of the waistband of his sweatpants. "I failed again. Your little act didn't work."

"Act?"

"You were trying tough love, or whatever, to get me to fly out of spite."

I cringe. "I...read that different techniques can help a tricky situation."

He huffs and looks away at the waterfall. "Yeah, well, clearly not even the power of frustration can get me to fly."

"But that's where you're wrong!" He turns to me, and I beam. "Clay, you flew!"

"Huh?"

"Well, you floated. Just for the briefest moment. I saw it."

"Seriously?" He looks down at his hands then up at the tree where he jumped.

"I wouldn't lie to you!" We share a laugh and I tap his bare, muscled arms.

"So then, progress?"

"I think we're so close to you actually gliding! Motivation is the key!"

"Of course. It was so different from your usual book-based encouragement!" He looks away and smiles, and we're both revitalized with energy.

"I raised the stakes!" I whip out my notebook from my coat pocket and flip a page. "Heightened emotions...that could be the trick."

"Now how can we raise the stakes further?" He stretches his arms and looks away. "The waterfall?"

We take a few steps toward the gorge. No one is around, and the babbling brook below is all ours. I read online that in the summertime, some folks jump off the waterfall, so I know he won't die. "That might work," I remark. I visualize Clay pulling that paper airplane maneuver and leaping off the waterfall. With enough control, he could aim to land himself right on the rock where we started.

Or he could tumble into the water.

"Only if you want to, though."

"Hey, no fear. Trepidation didn't get me to hover just now, anger did." He grins and points at me, and I laugh.

"So what, you want me to make you upset?"

"No. Motivate me by raising the stakes further. Let's make this interesting." He bounces an eyebrow at me, and it's so sexy I don't register what he's saying.

"Um..."

"Owen, if I fall into the water, you get to kick me in the nuts."

"What?"

He sits down on a stump and he takes off his shoes and socks. Next—monster god help me—he stands up to take off his sweats.

My eyes go wide at the sight of him in the world's tightest pair of boxer briefs. I'm aware I've seen him naked and in swimming briefs, but each time I gaze at his body it's a miracle to behold.

"Wha...wha...what?" I stammer.

He smirks like he can read my mind. He walks up to me and forces the sweatpants into my hands. "If I fly, I get to steal a kiss from you." He winks and dashes off to the top of the waterfall.

I'm in shock by everything going on that his words go in one ear and out the other. He's far gone by the time I say, "Wait, *what*?"

I move closer to the ledge, and in seconds, he's at the top of the waterfall. He's majestic, standing there in almost no clothes, arms outstretched, and eyes closed. He's attuning himself to the various breezes over the waterfall.

I want him to succeed so badly. I want to see this vampire take flight for the first time. I want my friend, Clay, to finally fulfill his destiny.

He looks up at the sky, and I smile at the sight. The memory of his most recent words finally hits me. If he accomplishes this, he...gets to kiss me?

Before I can properly panic, I watch him jump. His arms are outstretched, and he floats in place like last time. Then, his body is diving down—shit, he's falling into the water. Disappointment forms in my gut, but a moment later, my emotions are thrown for a loop.

Clay Cannon flies right back up. With the momentum of his little dive, and his arms now at his sides like some sort of airborne torpedo, he's shooting upward. There is no denying that he's defying all gravity. When he reaches the apex, a few feet higher than the origin of the waterfall, he opens his arms again and freezes in place. Then, he gently glides forward, like a human kite.

My heart nearly bursts at the realization: this sexy vampire jock is at long last flying.

ELEVEN

CLAY

T he mist from the waterfall brushes my skin as I glide past it, and then I catch another gust of wind and spiral on up to the top of the trees.

Oh, hell yes. I'm, like, a superhero or something. Just one wearing boxer briefs instead of a rubber suit with a cape.

I let out a holler as I zoom down toward the river. I keep my feet together, my butt tucked in. I'm trying to have good form—like a dancer or a gymnast. I stretch my arms over my head like the Man of Steel, but then I spread them wide so I can bank a turn when the thermals spiral. A sense of freedom takes over my whole body. I can do anything.

Owen was correct. Not only can I fly—glide, whatever—but I'm *good* at it. I should've remembered that when I was a kid growing up in California, I used to go surfing. The first few times I tried to stand up on the board, I ate shit. I couldn't get the hang of how to catch the wave with the piece of fiberglass and how to balance my body on the board. I fell time and time again.

But once I figured it out, I'd soar down those waves, riding the currents until I made it to shore or fell off the surfboard. Then I'd do it again, and again, and again.

Gliding is the same thing. It's *air* surfing.

And Owen is the one who gave me this gift. My heart opens up to the little nerdy human. He's making me feel invincible.

I fly down to the river, letting it splash my face, then speed back up again.

The heightened emotions help, yeah, but now that I'm figuring out how the balance of this works, I'll be able to catch the currents again. I'll just have to practice more.

Knowing how to glide is a major weight off my shoulders, in more ways than one. It's not only that my body feels lighter, but the piece of me that's felt wrong or missing is just...absent. It's like I can finally relax in my own blue skin. Even though I already had vampire speed, this brings my powers to another level.

"Do it again!" Owen calls, and I oblige, soaring up to the top of the waterfall and then taking a leap off. This time I'm more graceful than my last attempt, and while I tell myself to not show off, I do anyway, trying a twist at the end.

Finally, I land next to him, my chest heaving and my soul happy.

Owen grins. "That was amazing!"

"It was! Thanks for your help! I guess insulting me is the way to motivate me."

He's totally checking out my abs. I know it.

He looks to the side, then focuses on my eyes. "Sorry about that. You know I didn't mean it. You're not worthless at all." He licks his lips, and while he's trying not to stare, he keeps looking at my mouth. He kicks at the ground. "So, I guess now...you're going to, like, call in your bet?"

I freeze for a moment, then shake my head. "Nah. It's all good."

Part of me can't believe I'm saying that. I really want to kiss him. My body temperature is so low that cool weather is quite comfortable to me, but feeling a warm-blooded human against my skin? That's the best.

What's more, I *like* this spunky nerd. But even I can read the room—err, forest—and I know he doesn't actually want to kiss me. Our bet was just motivation to get me to fly. Nothing more.

I never want to force him to do something he doesn't want to do. I can't forget the way he got the hell out of my dorm room when we got our wires crossed before. I may be slow, but I can learn.

Owen seems like he's going to say something, then presses his lips tight and nods a few times, breaking eye contact with me. His shoulders hunch, and he sighs heavily. "Um, yeah. Okay. Whatever you want." He rubs his arms and turns, then stumbles mid-stride. I catch him around the waist, and a zing passes between us where our bodies touch. I let him go quickly.

Did I read him wrong? Does he actually want to kiss me? I open my mouth to say I've changed my mind, but he's already crouched down, opening up Bat Nathanson's carrier. "Our familiar could watch you, but I think he's going to want to do his own soaring."

I grin. "I'll show him the ropes. Come on, little buddy. Let's see what you can do."

Unfortunately, BN flaps his wings a few times, but doesn't get far.

"There's no way we're going to heighten his emotions by yelling at him," I say.

"Never," Owen says fiercely. "He's our baby. We protect him."

After another minute of watching him fail to get anywhere, we put BN back in the carrier.

"Do you mind if I take to the sky one more time?" I ask.

"Not at all." Owen gives me a shooing motion, so I super-speed to the ledge again. I jump off and after diving down, I glide up into the sky.

The wind feels amazing. There's only one feeling better than flying—sex, obviously—but I'm not getting any of that any time soon. So I focus on riding the thermals until I land by Owen, content but exhilarated.

Well, content with flying. I just wish Owen would be as open to exploring things with me as I am with him.

WE RETURN to the hotel room, and I take a quick shower, needing to wash the river water off of me. I wrap a towel around my waist and enter our bedroom. Owen looks up at me and stares.

He's been playing on his phone, but he drops it on the bed as his jaw parts slightly. What a cutie. He likes me, he's just trying to hide it.

I hold out my arms. "Like what you see?"

Owen's cheeks darken. "Um..."

I flash my fangs. "Just messing with you, Bhat. I know you can't stand jocks.

"Um, right...can't stand jocks."

I don't need vampire hearing to realize that last sentence lacked conviction. Hmm, perhaps I'm not completely out of luck with this sexy nerd.

He gets up and fusses with Bat Nathanson. Since BN's nocturnal, we've taken to letting him out of his terrarium at night, which he seems to appreciate. Owen gives him some fresh water and a container of blood with a sippy straw.

Must be nice to have Owen caring for you.

The hotel room's pleasant enough, with two queen beds, a large television, and a sitting area off to the side. It's decorated in an understated, trendy, modern style. Being so close to the gorge, the environs are quiet and very peaceful.

I walk over to my luggage and fish out a pair of boxer briefs. I might as well not scandalize Owen further. I drop my towel but turn away from him so he doesn't get more of a glimpse of the bits than he wants.

"Do you need to sleep?" Owen asks, interested, as always, in my monster habits.

Tugging my underwear up my legs, I snap the waistband and walk my towel back into the bathroom so it can dry. "No," I call. "But I rest sometimes and it feels good to be in bed. Alone or with someone else. Mostly with someone, though."

I realize how that second part of the sentence sounds—like I want him in my bed, which of course, I do.

The thing is, though, while I'm really attracted to Owen, I want more than his body. I like his earnestness and intelligence. I like how enthusiastic he is about his studies. I've always liked bookish guys in general, but there's something special about Owen. He doesn't make me feel like I'm lacking in the brains department. He makes me feel like I'm more than just a loser vampire who took twenty years before I got my act together enough to go to college. He makes me feel... worthy.

Returning to the room, Owen's propped up in his bed, glasses perched on his nose, and a tablet open in front of him.

"Whatcha reading?" I ask.

"It's a scientific article on vampire flight, comparing it to vampire bat flight."

"Isn't it a tad late to be reading it?" I turn down the covers on my bed.

"Well, just because you can fly now doesn't mean you won't have further questions or can't improve."

"I meant that it's midnight." I motion to the light, and he nods, chuckling. I flip the switch.

"Oh, yeah. That. Yes." He sets his tablet down on the bedside table, removes his glasses, and places them next to it. Then he flops on his side, facing me. While it takes my eyes a moment to get used to the dark, I can see quite well. An advantage of being a bloodsucking monster, I guess.

I lie on my back and stare at the ceiling. It's smooth white paint, glowing in the faint light of the outside hall light, and really not very interesting. But I have to focus on something other than the hot-blooded male lying in the next bed over, before I fly over there—literally—and give him that kiss I won.

But I fail at shifting focus. All I'm thinking about is how I can feel his heat, even across the room. How I can hear his heartbeat speed up.

His breath is coming in quick pants.

He flips the sheet off of him.

I smell his arousal.

Monster god, I'm going to go over and do something I'll regret. Something he doesn't want me to do. Or something he *says* he doesn't want me to do. I'll respect his wishes.

The second he makes a move, though, I'm all over him.

It'll have to be up to him.

I flip over so my back is facing him, which is not at all how I want to be. But I don't know how else to shut him out. He's just too mouthwatering. My fangs are completely descended, my cock is thickening, and I'm dying for a taste of him.

But I can control my thirst. Both kinds—for his blood and his body.

I think.

I busy myself counting Owen's heartbeats, and while I don't

have a clock out, they seem to be going faster than seventy beats per minute. I start counting his heartbeats.

One, two, three...

100, 101, 102...

1,000, 1,001, 1,002...

A rustle in his bed.

Now I'm up to 1,862, 1,863, 1,864 heartbeats. So, it's been like eighteen minutes since I turned out the light, I think.

He shuffles his covers and swings his legs over the side of the bed. Maybe he has to go pee.

1,867, 1,868. His heart rate speeds even faster. 1,872, 1,873. Owen's feet pad across the carpeted floor.

Except, instead of going to the bathroom, he walks over to the side of my bed.

1,980.

I flop onto my back, acting like I was sleeping. "Hey," I say, doing my best to sound groggy. "What's up?"

1,993, 1,994. They're getting even faster.

"I...feel cheated," he whispers.

I grin, even though he can't see it. "Oh? How?"

"You said you'd kiss me. You...deserve your prize."

Hearing this makes my heart skip a beat.

What number was I on? It doesn't matter.

"Then c'mere and give it to me." Stretching my arm wide, I fling the sheet to the side. In an instant, Owen's climbed into bed, straddled my hips, and is now lowering his face to mine.

Owen is wearing a tight white tank top that shows off his physique. The waistband of his crimson red briefs peeks over the top of his plaid pajama bottoms. He smells sweet, and he's so warm, and his hair is messy and sexy.

I hold his face in both hands and bring my lips to his. He eagerly kisses me at the same time I kiss him back, and our touch alters something deep inside me.

His hot lips on my cold ones, his desperate tongue in my mouth, the way he's now leaning down and tugging my hair. The fact that I can feel his hard dick rubbing against my torso.

I can hear his throbbing veins—in his neck, and in his cock.

Monster god, I want him.

"Can I touch you?" I ask, wanting to be sure, since he was all "no jocks" earlier.

"Fuck, yes," he whispers, his voice hoarser, as he takes off his shirt. Instantly, my hands are tracing his bare back, sliding down to his round, perfect ass.

He moans.

"Are my hands too cold?" I whisper. My fangs want to sink into him, but I can hold back. I think.

"No, I like them. I'm always too hot."

Our kisses turn more frantic. I sit up with my back to the headboard and pull Owen with me so he's still straddling my lap.

Now I want to make him come. I want to release all this tension I've been feeling inside for him.

He's going to be mine. I just know it.

Except...as much as I want to fucking own him, I need to dial it back. He's human and therefore much more fragile than I am. Plus, I usually deny myself human feeders, choosing instead to just drink blood from a plastic bag.

I want his blood. Monster *god*, I want it.

I'm at an advantage here, because I can see him perfectly while he can't see me as well, I'm sure. Not only do I see better in the dark, but he's not wearing his glasses.

"You're so gorgeous," I mutter, trailing a fingertip down his chest.

He shivers under me, but I think it's from arousal, not my body temperature. Or maybe it's both. His skin feels molten hot under my touch. He grinds his dick against my side. "Fuck," he hisses. "I need...more."

"Just so you know," I say, holding his chest and seeking out his eyes, even though he can't see me. "They say vampires aren't supposed to be able to get STIs or transmit them, but I still get tested, and I'm negative. I don't want you to worry."

"Yeah," he pants. "I'm negative too."

"Then let's get these off," I whisper, hooking my fingers in the waistband of his briefs.

Owen nods a few times and adjusts his position to make it so we can slide them down.

And now, this handsome man is sprawled over me, fully naked and completely aroused. "Wet dreams are made of this," I admit, running my fingers down his rounded shoulders, wiry arms, narrow hips, and then his hairy thighs.

"Make me come, Clay," Owen growls, losing patience, and I grin.

"With pleasure." I scoot under him so I'm on my back. "Fuck my face."

"You...you sure?"

"Yep. Then you can control how deep you go. Just watch out for my fangs."

"*Fuck*," Owen groans again, as he changes his position, lining his hot, hard dick up with my waiting mouth.

I open wide, and he slides in, tentative at first. "Oh, fuck, oh fuck," he moans. "This feels so good. It's cool, but so wet and the suction is so tight, and oh my monster god."

He holds on to the top of the headboard above me and tilts his angle so he's on his knees on either side of me, his dick fucking my throat.

I reach down and grab his ass, encouraging him to go deeper, faster, longer. To make me choke, which is almost impossible to do, given my monster skills.

I can taste his precum and smell his sweat. I love all of it.

"Oh, monster god," Owen starts chanting, picking up his speed. I can't talk, but I hope I'm communicating how much I want him to use me with how I'm guiding his ass toward my mouth, gripping it hard.

When he seems to get the idea and takes over at a brutal pace I love, I keep one hand on his hip and with the other, reach down to stroke my own cock.

How badly do I want to bury it inside his hot body? On a scale of one to ten, it's twenty million.

But he's not ready for that, I don't think.

Secret hookups in the dark can turn into other things in the light of day.

For now, Owen's getting close. His balls are drawing up closer to his body, and his thrusts are getting artless. My mouth feels abused, which is exactly the way I prefer it—for my jaw to ache, my breathing to be labored. For it all to be too much.

I can sense when Owen's going to pull back, but I want him to finish inside my mouth. So I hold his ass to me, his cock down my throat so far I'd choke if I were still human.

"Clay...I'm about to..." His voice goes higher, and I love the way he says my name. A moment later, it happens: with a shout, he starts pulsing into me. His hot, salty release warms my insides and gives me a jolt of energy like a breakfast shot of blood.

After a few more aftershocks, he pulls out and collapses to the side, reaching out a hand for my cock, which I've been inter-mittently neglecting.

I bat his hand away, choosing to jack myself, but he holds his mouth open over my tip, clearly communicating that he wants to help.

Fine by me. I let him suck me, and with Owen licking my cock, I tip over into the realm of brain blackouts and full-body shakes, the orgasm hitting me hard. How long has it been since I last came?

Once my body calms down, I tug him up onto me and give him a kiss. "Seems I won my bet after all."

He cuddles into me.

"Did you know that for vampires, semen is a form of sustenance? If we can't get blood, we can, you know, suck cock," I say.

He snickers. "That is *not* true."

"How would you know? How do you know I don't feel invigorated right now, having given you a blow job?"

"Do you really feel that way?" Owen asks with a grin.

"Definitely."

"Splendiferous. I love learning more about monsters." Owen's voice is dreamy, and soon enough he's falling asleep against my chest.

TWELVE

OWEN

The thrum of Clay's car on the highway vibrates through my feet into my body. I'm holding our pet in the towel-covered terrarium on my lap, an almost identical scene from yesterday. Everything between us has changed, but that's what happens when you have the best oral sex hookup of your life with your monster lab partner. We're both quiet, opting instead to listen to whatever's on the radio on the road back to Creelin.

He smiles at me from the driver's seat, and I smile too. We decidedly don't talk about it.

Neither of us mentioned our night together when I woke up in his arms. We each got ready and checked out promptly so we could get back to school on time. I'm still waiting for him to say anything of substance. I keep imagining the vampire saying, *"Great sex last night, Owen, I'm so glad you rescinded your 'No sex with jocks' rule. Wanna get some toasted boo-gels with scream cheese?"*

But no, we barely converse, both of us opting to make small talk about the funny billboards we see on the drive. And BN is once again asleep in my lap, so the status quo is back to where it should be. I guess our tryst is to remain a secret; what happens in Stokerbram Park stays in Stokerbram Park, I suppose.

This is good, though. I have to focus on my pre-med major, and Clay has some water polo stuff presumably. No distractions for either of us, and jocks have always been heartbreak waiting to happen. Our intimate hookup was just a reward for him taking to the skies for the first time, a sexy little prize for both of us. There are no feelings to be had; it's not as if it filled me with delight to see him achieve his goal of gliding, and it's not like watching him be a co-parent is a beautiful miracle to behold.

If I say the words enough in my head, I'll believe it.

HE DRIVES up to the parking area near my dorm and stops the car. I smooth out the towel on the terrarium just to bide my time.

"I had a great weekend," he says in a low tone.

"It um...we accomplished a lot," I reply.

"Yeah." I turn and gaze at his precious eyes as he continues, "But, uh, I still have a lot to learn."

"Do you?"

"Yeah. I need to learn how to fly in less windy environments. Plus, I want to be able to glide with clothes on."

The memory of his cock from last night flares through my head and down to my groin. "Um, yeah."

"And we need to teach Bat Nathanson how to fly."

"Very true," I say, gripping the box tighter. "You good to take him back? Need me to help?"

"No, I got it. I have plenty of blood for him at my place."

"Splendid," I murmur. Why does my heart feel so disappointed?

"So, I'll uh...hit you up for the next flying lesson?"

I nod. "We should probably study for the next anatomy quiz."

"Oh right, all about humans." He shrugs. "I mean, I am human. Well, at least I was for twenty years."

"But we could still help each other!" I remark.

"Sounds like a plan. You got my number, Bhat." He leans back and smirks. "Use it."

I nod and focus on getting out of the car without disturbing our familiar. My cheeks prickle at the idea of Clay pronouncing my last name correctly. I buckle up the terrarium, grab my luggage, and walk away.

I only turn around once to see his car drive across campus. Our weekend hookup wasn't a big deal—so then why does the prospect of our next study session fill me with satisfaction?

"Hey, come on in."

"Hey, man." Clay enters my dorm and looks around. It's been a week since he flew around the waterfall and we had sex. I've been going to class and taking care of Bat Nathanson, and everything has been platonic as ever. We planned to have this crash course on human anatomy today.

"Welcome, to, uh, Casa de Owen. Population, moi." I cringe at the terms I just used, but Clay doesn't seem to notice, opting to look around instead. I play with my hands and fastidiously fix the bed, wondering if any post-studying adult activities might occur.

Oh, who am I kidding—half of the reason I invited him here is to have a no-strings-attached oral intercourse session. But only if he's interested.

"So, where's your roommate?" Clay asks, putting down his backpack. He sits at my desk near my open laptop and textbook.

"He went home for the weekend." I gaze at my lab partner; he looks delicious as ever in his athletic zip-up hoodie and jeans, and I hope I look just as good in a green T-shirt and pajama pants.

"So, it's just us, eh?" Clay bounces that eyebrow at me, and I know a playboy like him knows what he's doing.

"Yup!" I yelp. I wipe my palms on my pants and try to will my erection down. "For, um...strictly studying." I point at him and chuckle for no reason.

"Right." His eyes deflate in disappointment. He opens his notebook and looks forward at my laptop. "It sucks that water polo practice went late and I missed most of the lecture."

"That does suck." I bring the other chair close to him and take a seat.

"But I have a brilliant lab partner who took notes." His voice is dripping with innuendo and he bounces that eyebrow again. That's almost as sexy as his fangs. My sheer proximity to him in my tiny dorm has my blood racing.

"You've already had sex," a sinister voice says in my mind. *"Just ask him again, he'll assuredly say yes."*

Clay unabashedly looks me up and down. Can vampires read minds?

"Um!" I hop up and push my chair back. Clay doesn't seem fazed at all by my little outburst.

"I need to uh, use the bathroom!" I announce in a high tone.

"Okay," he replies, coolly. "Can I catch up on the notes while I wait?"

"Totally, totally, one-hundred-and-ten percent!" *Why did I just say that?* I unlock my laptop and pull up a folder of presentations, all while cringing.

A minute later, I'm in the dorm communal bathroom. Fortunately, I'm alone as I take a leak, wipe my dick, wash my face, and give myself a little pep talk in the mirror. "It's just studying...with a...vampire stud," I mutter. I put my glasses on, pat my hair down, and quickly walk back to my room.

When I enter, the sight makes the blood drain from my face —Clay is scrolling through the presentation I made two months ago as a joke. He's watching photos of dudes zoom by while my slides tell about how hot I find vampires.

"Um...what are you...?" I crowd the desk but not before he clicks to the next slide.

"Wait, is that me?"

I can hear his smirk as I hurriedly try to turn off the presentation. "Um, that was nothing, just an—"

"You made that about me?"

"No! What? Huh? I don't know who made that!" My lies are bringing my voice higher while I desperately try to click on anything to turn it off. *Why isn't the escape button working?*

"Well, it said 'by Owen Bhat' at the very beginning..."

Fuck it. I shut my laptop and push it away. Then I lean on the desk with one hand and try to give my best "everything is fine" smile while I catch my breath.

Clay, meanwhile, looks deeply amused. None of my terrible bluffs are getting through to this gorgeous vampire jock. He's so smug right now, I can't stand him.

"Forget about lectures, I can just...dictate to you about human anatomy. I am human after all." I shrug and pull up the chair.

"All right."

"So, let's see." I take out my notebook and push up my glasses. "The human muscular system. Most monsters share the same anatomy, and Octavia pointed out how important it is for pre-med students."

"Is that what you want to do?"

The sincerity in his voice gives me pause. I notice his handsome face inches from mine, and I bite my lip. "Yeah. I want to be a doctor for monsters."

"That's really noble," he says.

I nod and look down, trying not to blush. "Right. Well, let's see what we focused on..." I gaze down at my notes. "You know about biceps?"

"I sure do." He pokes my arm with the blunt end of his pen, and that simple contact has me chubbing up.

I swallow. "Well, did you know there's a biceps femoris?"

"There is?"

"Oh yeah, it's um..." A naughty thought rises in my brain, and for the first time in my life, I try not to overthink things. *Just go for it, Owen.* "It's right above the soleus."

I stand up and drop my pants revealing my tight green boxer briefs. I step out of my pants and slippers and ignore Clay's eyes on me. When I place my bare foot on the chair, I point down. "Remember where the soleus is?"

When I look at Clay, I notice his gaze is blown wide open. He's not smirking anymore, and I don't even think he's breathing. "Um...right there," he murmurs. He points at the area above my ankle, and I once again feel the sparks.

"Correct," I say with a grin. "And do you remember the name of the superficial muscle above it?"

He looks me up and down, and the energy in the room is charged between us. I didn't realize our study session would get so naughty so quickly. "It's uh...g-g-gastrocnemius."

"Great job, Cannon." I take his hand and bring it up farther, right behind my thigh. "Now, biceps femoris is...about here."

"H-h-here," he stammers.

I grin—I've got this vampire right where I want him.

"Silly me, you can't see anything at this angle," I say with a faux-chastisement. "Come here."

I beckon him to stand by the bed. Then, in my boldest move yet, I take off my shirt and lie on my back. With my bent knees, I lift up one leg. "Can you see it now?"

"Um...uh huh!" His voice is higher, and I swear he's drooling.

"Touch it," I command. He visibly gulps and leans forward. When he taps behind my thigh, I take the opportunity to put my ankle on his shoulder.

"Good job."

"Th...th-thanks," he stammers.

"Any other...muscles you want to review from here?"

"Just, um...yeah..." I don't think he's blinked in five minutes.

"Well, this..." I bring his hand along to above my thigh. "...is quadriceps femoris."

"Quadriceps...femoris," he whispers. His fingers are cold, but the slight skin-on-skin contact has my blood boiling.

"And this..." I drag it close to my inner thigh. My balls tingle and my cock twitches against the thin fabric of my underwear. "This is the adductor muscle."

"Adductor," he says in a raspy tone. It's like his eyes don't know where to stay, my shirtless body, my thighs, or my crotch.

We stay like this for a long, quiet moment, my ankle on his shoulder. He lightly traces my adductor muscle, and my dick and balls go wild. "You're triggering my reflex," I murmur.

"What?"

"Haven't you heard about cremasteric reflex?"

"What's that?" His voice is a low growl, and yes, his fangs are out. He could devour me right now, and I'd probably say thank you.

"It's not on the syllabus," I say. "Stroking the inner thigh of a human male...you know what it does?"

"Wha...what?"

I gaze right at him and drag his hand up and down my inner thigh. "It makes...the testicles elevate."

"Really?" His voice is a whisper again, and I'm afraid his eyebrows will never go down.

"Yeah, wanna see?"

"Um...if you don't mind."

I move my leg down and he steps back. In a blur, my boxer briefs are gone, and I'm naked on the bed. Clay takes the moment to ditch his hoodie and shirt, and he's back to crowding my groin.

I hike my ankle back up onto his right shoulder so he can access me more easily. Then, I take his hand again, and slowly, glacially, I bring his fingers back to my right inner thigh. My hard cock is so close to him, but I don't want to take that final step just yet.

"Watch," I whisper. I make his hand stroke my thigh, and right on time, my low-hangers go up and down.

"Amazing," he says with pure wonder. His adoration makes my pulse race faster. No one's ever made me feel this attractive before. You would think we didn't hook up a week ago.

"It sure is."

"Does it hurt?"

I purse my lips. "No. But it, like, stimulates my dick."

"Really?"

"Yeah. You never felt it before?"

"No." He continues to stroke my skin and study my balls. "I guess I lost it when I turned into a vampire."

"Ah." We stay that way for a minute more, him sinfully making the lightest circle on my inner thigh. The delicate touch naturally makes my nuts twitch, but it's bringing delicious sensations to my hardness too. My cock demands more attention, but I'm loving the feel of this feathery caress.

"Wow," he whispers.

"Yup." I grin. "The only problem is if you do that enough I'll end up with a proper case of blue balls."

I chuckle, but he looks at me so seriously. "I...never want to hurt you."

"It's not a big deal," I reply, waving my hand away.

"I can...help you." He brings his hand closer and caresses my sack. I'm so glad I shaved my pubes yesterday, and the simple contact sends more shivers up my spine.

He grasps just the base of my dick and it instantly goes full mast. I let out a breathy sigh and roll my head around on the bed. "O...only if you want to, Clay."

"It's the polite thing to do," he murmurs. When he traces my length, a tiny drop of precum oozes out, and my whole body lights on fire.

"Okay," I whisper, not wanting to forbear this sexual contact any longer. I shut my eyes and—

He's stroking me. Damn, Clay is stroking me, and it feels so good.

"Uhh," I rasp. I sigh and my hips instinctively thrust up.

"You like that?" he murmurs.

When I open my eyes, the sight nearly has me losing all control. "Fuck yes," I whisper. Clay is stroking me, and he's working my cock almost reverently.

I've never been worshipped before, but there are a lot of nevers that Clay Cannon has brought into my life.

"Would it be rude to say you...are so fucking sexy, Owen?" He kisses the tip of my cock, and more fluid leaks out.

"Ah...no, not at all," I say in a whiny, breathy tone. With my ankle up, he has my ass exposed. If I had prepared myself at all, I'd beg him to fuck me, but I don't think I'm ready for that in several ways. Besides, the way he's jerking me has me seeing stars. I hiss as he picks up the pace, and I want to ask him, no, *beg* him, for more.

"Can I suck you?" he whispers. I almost don't hear it over the crackle of his hand, slick with precum, gliding up and down.

"Yes," I reply in a raspy tone. In the next moment, my cock is reunited with Clay's wanting mouth. Like last time, his oral sex game is extraordinary. This isn't a hurried affair in the dark, we're taking our time. This study session has become so much more.

Study, what studying? What are classes? I don't remember my own name as Clay takes my cock all the way down his throat.

Looking up at him as he slowly services me is overwhelming. His eyelashes are huge, and they make his piercing gaze even sexier. Up and down he goes, not even gagging. My cock, hell, my whole body is transcending to another realm.

If sex with Clay is always like this, I'd be down to fool around with this vampire for years to come.

"Fuh, Clay," I murmur as I grip the sheets.

"Mm," he says. The vibrations go up my spine, and he doesn't stop for a beat. He's never too firm, too soft, too fast, and definitely not too slow. Clay plays my cock like it's an instrument he's been practicing his whole life. If being in his forties made him this good at oral, I can't wait to have him completely inside me.

"Fuck," I utter. He caresses my balls, and it's all too much. "Almost..."

"Yeah?" he asks when he pulls off momentarily.

"Yes," I rasp through a sigh.

"Mm," he replies, mouth full of cock again. Up and down he goes, and after a few seconds, I moan, letting him know I'm about to explode.

Heaven. That's the only way I can describe it as Clay gives me an orgasm for the second time. A guttural noise escapes my lips as I climax. I shoot and shoot, and Clay speeds up his sucking, then slows down at the right time.

I come back down from paradise and look up to see him wiping his mouth. He gently puts my leg down, and I'm touched to see he's being so polite. He grins and flashes those perfect fangs. Between that, the abs, the chest, and glossy mouth, I can barely stay away from him.

"We should probably go—"

"Oh no we don't," I say. Faster than I ever have, I leap off the mattress and get down to my knees. I undo his pants and force him onto the bed. When his hardness springs forth, I grin.

"My turn." I lean in and kiss his balls, reveling in his manly scent, a hint of pine mixed with pool water. I look up and raise my eyebrows, wordlessly asking for consent.

He's in shock, so I push up my glasses and lick my lips. "Fuck, please," he rasps, throwing his head back.

I knew he liked my glasses. Not wanting to overthink anything, I lean forward and take him in. The dude is thick and long, and admittedly, I gag when I take him to the back of my throat. But Clay doesn't seem to care, moaning and sighing like the dorm walls aren't thin.

He cards his fingers through my curls, and I suck and suck. I lick the uncut head clean and keep going down. I play with his balls just like he did mine and try to keep his cock nice and wet as I take him into me.

"Owen...shit...Owen," his voice rises, and I know he's right there. I swallow, suck, stroke, and swallow again. In a few moments, he erupts in my mouth, and I gulp it all down. I've never been greedy for semen before, but this is the hot vampire water polo jock I've been lusting after—he's the exception to all my rules.

After a minute, since Clay doesn't get up—he's so strung out, so I'm patting myself on the back for a blow job well done—I lie in bed with him. We've cuddled before, why not do it again?

I stroke his firm chest with my left hand, and he turns to his left to gaze at me. It's quiet, and we're both breathing softly.

"In the interest of academics and actually learning..." I say in a scratchy tone.

"Yeah?"

"We should probably study in the library next time."

With that, we both end up in a laughing fit, here in my bed. I've never smiled this much with a sexual partner before—yet another never that Clay Cannon has brought into my world.

CHAPTER

THIRTEEN

CLAY

Today, I'm hanging with the water polo team because of our exhibition game against Packard U.

I'm standing at my locker in the Creelin U Athletics Center, pulling my Speedo on. As I slide the tiny fabric up my muscular, hairy thighs, I think about how a week ago, Owen taught me parts of the body I've never known about.

Since then, I've thought about those body parts plenty—in between classes, when I'm swimming, late at night when Owen's asleep in his dorm room and I'm restless in my own bed. I've jacked off so much to thoughts of what we've done together, but it doesn't help. My thirst for him has become insatiable.

What does his blood taste like? That's been a dominant thought. That, and how to get him naked as many times as I can, as often as I can. But while I enjoy spending time with him studying and caring for our familiar, my bloodlust is starting to become overpowering. In fact, I've taken to getting double blood bags at the cafeteria in the morning and afternoon instead of my usual amount. It's like I'm trying to fill up something inside when Owen's not around.

But then, he'll text me, and either I'll glide over or he'll come to my room, and we'll hook up. Those few times, it's felt... destined. Like Owen and I are meant to be together. Everything feels right when he's around.

I'm worried because as we grow closer, I crave his blood more. It's getting harder and harder for me to keep from sinking my fangs into his hot, velvety flesh and feeding from him. Giving him blowjobs and drinking his release does satiate me a little bit, but I'm wanting more.

I'm never going to allow myself to have it. I can't risk having feelings for him, and I also don't want to hurt him, physically. So Owen's never going to be my feeder. I have to accept that.

Stewing with these thoughts has made me way less outgoing than I usually am. Someone's noticed.

"Where have you been?" Brandon demands, as he slams his locker door shut. He's wearing his steel necklace that prevents him from being drowned by his boyfriend's scream. It also protects the entire team, so the officials let him wear it, even though it can get tugged on quite a bit. "I hardly see you outside of practice these days."

"And barely even then," Nick says—so, make that two someones—his Scottish lilt coming out more than usual. Nick must've been talking with his parents. His accent always gets thicker after a long session with them.

The nøkk's in his monster form, with gray and mossy skin, but his eyes are always the same. He joins Brandon, picking up their towels. Maybe I should talk with the nøkk about how he fights his desire to take Bran's soul. I'm in the same boat, because damn, I want to feed from Owen so badly it's starting to affect me. I need to drink from his throat, or suck his dick every day, or both.

I rub the back of my neck. "I'm...around. Going to class. Taking care of a bat. You know, the usual."

Bran gasps and points at my face. "Oh my god, you're seeing someone."

"How did you get that from 'the usual'?" I ask with a frown.

"Because if you were just hooking up like normal, I'd be hearing about it in between and seeing you. You must be dating someone. Who is it?"

I take a deep breath in and out, and my shoulders slump. "My lab partner," I admit.

"Owen Bhat?" Nick asks.

I whip my head over to him. "How do you know his name?" What I really want to do is to snarl that he should get Owen's pretty name out of his mouth. That's probably not the wisest way to act toward my teammate before a game.

"Owen's a good guy. And you must be making his dreams come true since he made that little HowlerPoint on you." Nick eyes me knowingly.

I grin despite myself, having now seen the presentation in question. "He's...cute, but I'm not sure we're dating. Monster-human relationships are complicated, man. Not that I have a relationship with Owen. We've hooked up a few times, that's all. Sure, I want more. We're...lab partners with benefits."

"That's not a thing," Bran points out. "And you like him. You just said you want more."

I lay a hand over my heart and close my eyes. "I'm not going to deny it."

"I want to meet him," Bran says.

"He said he'd be here."

"Awesome."

I hope it will be.

THE TEAM FILES OUT to the pool area from the locker room, and we do our usual warm-up routine. It's humid inside, and the whole place smells like salt. The opposing team has a merman —they're always hard to defend. But we have a nøkk as a goalie, and he's excellent.

My mind isn't on the game. It's on who I spot sitting in the stands.

First row, next to the stairs, you can't miss him. Owen sits with BN on the bleachers, raptly watching us.

Or rather, watching me.

The game's not starting for another ten minutes, so I get out of the water and pad over to him, dripping wet. "Hey! Glad you could come watch!"

"Hey," Owen says with a smile.

BN sits in his lap and says, "Squeak!"

"Hey, little buddy," I say, and go to pet his head, but I'm wet so I pull back. The move gets me closer to Owen, though, who stares up and down my body. I guess I do look good, my muscles tight from exercise and water streaming down my body. This scrap of fabric barely covers my junk, and it shows off all that anatomy Owen was reciting two weeks ago.

"Are you going to tell me where my different muscles are?" I ask in a low voice near his ear. His warm skin is just right there, ready for me to bite.

He coughs and shuffles his feet. "Don't make me hard while I'm watching you."

I pointedly look at his crotch. "Don't threaten me with a good time." My own dick is starting to strain against my bathing suit, so I'll need to think of something not sexy to make it go back down.

"Cannon, get back in the pool," Coach Rosmarus yells. Coach is a walrus shifter, and not my type at all. That'll do it.

I wink at Owen and trot over to the rest of the team, hopping in the water.

Brandon swims over to me. "That's your guy? The one with the glasses?"

"Yep." My brain likes the phrase, *your guy*.

"He's cute. You've always liked the nerdy ones."

I splash water in his face.

WE WIN THE EXHIBITION GAME, in part because I score five goals. On some level, I think I was showing off because Owen was in the stands. In fact, I know I was.

After the game, when I'm showered and dry, Owen's waiting for me outside. I swiftly steal a kiss from him, and he looks momentarily stunned but not completely vexed. We haven't defined any relationship, and that was definitely a boyfriend thing to do. But I don't care. He's mine.

"You played really well," he says. I gesture for him to pass over BN, and he hands me the carrying case.

"Thanks. The game was fun. We have a few scrimmages and other exhibition games until the training starts again this summer."

"Do you want to study this weekend?"

"I do, but the Vampire Gliding Enthusiasts asked me to go with them. Again. I agreed, but I'm thinking of canceling."

"But you put in all that work so that you'd be able to do it," he points out.

"Trying to get rid of me, Bhat?"

"No, not at all. I just want you to reap the rewards of your hard work."

"Then I'll go," I say. "For you. But I'll meet you right after."

Brandon comes trotting up with the nøkk in tow. Steve's returned to his emo human form. Bran's holding Steve's hand, but he lets go of it to offer his hand to Owen to shake. "Hey, I'm Brandon Fernandez, Clay's best friend."

Owen gives me a look that says, *why haven't I met your best friend before?* "Oh? Nice to meet you."

"He hasn't talked about me, has he?"

"Are you the one who texts in emojis?" Owen asks.

Bran nods a few times with a huge smile on his face. "That's me!"

"He's mentioned you. All good things."

"And this is Steve, my boyfriend," Bran says.

Steve holds out his hand. "It is nice to meet you, Owen." While Steve's loosened up a bit being with Bran, he can still be pretty formal.

"Likewise."

"Catch you guys later," Bran says, and he scoots off, the nøkk at his side.

"They seem nice," Owen says.

"They're great. Maybe we can go get some food with them later. Or just you and me."

Owen's cheeks darken as usual whenever I say something that makes him embarrassed or aroused.

But that also makes his blood flow to the surface, and I'm going to need to get a move on. He's just too tempting, and I want to take him right here outside the pool complex. Which is a very bad idea, especially when I'm supposed to be flying. I kiss him goodbye and book it over to where I'm meeting the club for instructions on our outing.

A few days later, I'm walking out with Shannon, Ray, and the rest of the Vampire Gliding Enthusiasts from the parking lot to the trailhead that leads us to the overlook at Shelley Mary Nature Reserve. A month ago, I never would've gone on this field trip. But now that I have some confidence in my ability to glide—aided by a few good pushes from Owen—I decided not to cancel.

Except I'm not used to flying without Owen around, and I'm feeling a little faint. My muscles are twitchy. This could be bad. I don't think I can do this.

I should've canceled.

I give everyone a tight smile as we get out of the vans.

"Ready?" Shannon asks. "I'm so excited!"

Everyone claps. "This is going to be a great session!" one of them hoots.

I've got a rolling feeling in my stomach. I don't even get this nervous before water polo games. But with those, I know what I'm doing.

With this outing...my nerves aren't just from the fact that I could get hurt. I'm more concerned that I could embarrass myself.

Maybe that will never go away.

Since we all move at vampire speed, it doesn't take us long to get to the edge, the takeoff site.

"Not sure why you haven't come out with us before," Ray says, knocking my shoulder with his as we survey the view. Trees, rocks, a stream below—admittedly, it's pretty.

But there's no wind today. I touch my ear. "I'm not into

group activities," I lie. Because what is water polo but a group activity?

Can I even do this without Owen? I've been gliding, but most of the time it's to see him, and maybe steal a kiss.

"Oh, gliding is more fun in a group. We can really catch the thermals." Ray gives me a wink, then spreads his arms out and falls backward off the cliff, gliding easily along.

The others jump off the ridge after him, easily moving, even with little wind.

"Here goes nothing, Cannon," I mutter to myself.

Here goes me falling flat.

Here goes me amounting to nothing, just like my parents said.

But then I think of Owen's face. *He believes in me.*

I can do this. Even with barely a breeze.

Closing my eyes, I clench all the muscles in my body. It's a long way down if I fall.

No. I can do this.

I bend my knees and picture Owen pushing up his glasses. I picture what it looks like when he's taking off his shirt. When he's kissing me.

Then I spring into the air, my body suddenly light.

Shannon zooms by me. "Woo-hoo!" she calls.

I chase after her, laughing, as my body adapts to gliding and I fly through the forest.

Thank you, Owen, for helping me.

FOURTEEN

OWEN

Trying to study in my room in the middle of the day is a lost cause. Fortunately, in my classes, I am essentially ahead of the curve and getting all A's. Otherwise I'd be concerned by my lack of concentration. Attempting to memorize the different types of blood cells only reminds me of bloodsuckers, which of course reminds me of a certain sexy water polo dude. He's away on some vampire day trip, which is good, otherwise I might scrape up some sad excuse to see him.

The past two weeks, we've been hooking up at least twice in the middle of the week. Usually we're studying, and then, bam! —the craving strikes both of us, and clothes are flying off. I've never had a friend-with-benefits before. I've also never had oral sex and cuddled with anyone as hot as Clay. Or any monster really. *All these nevers...*

I sigh and slowly shut my book so as to not wake up Bat Nathanson. I glance at the towel-covered terrarium taking up most of my desk. My familiar has been so good, quietly mulling about when my roommate, Michael, and I sleep, and of course, snoozing during the day. I've grown so fond of the little fella, and a selfish part of me hopes he never leaves the metaphorical nest.

I wonder what my parents would think if they found out I have a familiar. They might accuse the infamous Creepin U of turning me into a witch, or some other ridiculous notion.

My phone buzzes and I quickly push the silence button. Seeing the name, I power-walk out of the room so I don't wake up the bat. I swipe and whisper, "Hello?"

"Owen? Owen, can you hear us?"

"Yes, Mom, hi. I was just studying in my dorm."

"It's the middle of the day. Don't you have classes?"

I walk to a hallway near the dorm elevator and gaze out the massive floor-to-ceiling window. "Sometimes. But not today at this hour."

"Ah."

"What's up?"

"We wanted to hear from you, right, Dad?"

I hear my dad bristle away from the phone. "Hi, Dad. You guys need anything?"

"Can't a mother call her son?"

I wince at the guilt. "You sure can."

"Here I thought you were, as the kids say, ghosting us."

I try not to roll my eyes. "That's...not what that means."

"Anyway, how are you, beta? Are you eating enough human food?"

This time my eyes do move. "All food in the dining hall is human food." Mostly true, but she doesn't need to know that.

"We just wanted to check up on you. You rarely answer our texts. And in the news I read all about monster kids involuntarily shifting. It's very scary."

I grit my teeth and gaze at an incubus walking around campus, shifting his form. "It's not scary, Mom."

"Don't some of those monster types drink blood?"

I huff. "Yeah, but we're made of blood."

"That's all the more reason to be afraid! Owen, your class-mates might eat you."

My patience is wearing thin. "They won't. And if you visited me, you'd know that."

"Your frightening school is three hours away."

The thought of them popping up renders me the slightest bit anxious. "On second thought, that's way too far, Mom. Basically four hours with traffic. Anyway, how's Auntie?"

Once again, I've successfully managed to divert the conversation. Mom talks all about her cousins, and I mostly just hum affirmations. We don't discuss how scary monsters are or how disappointed they are that I'm not at a human university. I just need to endure for a few more years and become the professional I want to be, and then my parents will have no choice but to accept my life.

"Aw, he just yawned at me!" Shonda coos as Bat Nathanson lies down on her palm.

"Yup, he just woke up." I grin at my friend as she delicately observes the mammal in her hands. It's late in the evening here at Mummy Mocha, the café inside the library building. Between the gold-and-yellow faux Egyptian motifs and the constant whir of coffee machines, it's a relaxing, popular spot for us students. Of course, having an actual student mummy as the manager makes it less "offensive caricature of ancient Egypt" and more "fun, themed hangout spot." The mummy shifter in question, Seth, is ringing up customers several feet away, while Shonda and I sit in a corner booth.

"Nocturnal, obviously." Shonda snickers and holds him up. "I keep thinking they're just like human vampires."

"Nope, they're very different." I sip on my tea and watch as my pet hops up and down on Shonda's palm. "However their diet consists of blood, hence the namesake. In fact, vampire bats predate the Halloween Wave. Therefore, technically, they were named after a creature that became real after the fact. A true chicken-and-egg scenario. Ha!"

I chuckle at my own joke but Shonda gives me that incredulous look she saves only for me. She and I have gotten along well since we met at human transfer orientation back in August, so she should be used to my admittedly tangential monster-themed ramblings.

She continues to let Bat Nathanson hop from one hand to another. We both grin at the little guy, entertained by his dance in the air. "Well, in any case, I can't believe you have your own familiar."

"I know. I never had pets growing up, but the tiny bat kind of loves us."

"Us?"

"I mean, me." I clear my throat. My friends have no idea that I've grown increasingly close to a campus jock. To be fair, I've never had the urge to talk about anyone's love life, let alone my own.

I mean, sex life. Just, some oral sex between lab partners, no love on the radar at all.

Shonda fixes a curious gaze on me, so I pick up the bat. "Hey, check this out. Bat Nathanson, can you say hello to Shonda?"

My pet nods and then squeaks.

"Aww," she coos, leaning into him. Crisis averted.

"I'd be happy to babysit this guy," she says.

I shake my head and smile. "He's pretty attached, I don't think he'll want to be watched by anyone else, to be honest."

Shonda sits back. "That's for the best. I don't think my suitemates will want a bat squeaking around at night."

"He's actually very quiet. But that may be because we keep him comfortable." I cough. "And by we, I mean, the, um, student population in general."

Shonda quirks an eyebrow, then remarks, "I'm surprised they let pets other than, like, service animals on campus."

"I was surprised, too. I thought untrained creatures had to stay outdoors," I reply.

"Hey, that is not true." We turn to look up and see Seth with an easy smile on his face. He's wearing a blue shirt with a white apron tied around his trim waist. With his ochre skin and easy smile, I understand why all the boys lust after him.

He sits next to me and adds, "We let Blake on campus, and he's the most untrained creature of all."

"Hey!" His friend Blake approaches us and slaps Seth on the head, and we all laugh. "Rude mummy asshole."

"You're the one who leaves beer bottles all over the suite!" Seth smirks at Blake, and I recall that they're best friends with Kovi. The fair-skinned dude with wild brown curls pulls up a chair and turns to us. "What's up, guys?"

"Check out Owen's familiar!" Shonda says.

They all fawn over Bat Nathanson, and I swear he preens. *Is this thing an animal from a Disney cartoon?*

"So cute," Seth says.

"I heard a human had a familiar on campus," Blake says, sipping his coffee.

"And I heard all sorts of...other rumors," Seth adds. He looks at me with that piercing brown stare. As the coffee guru, I figured he was the campus gossip, but does he know just how much Clay and I have done?

I clear my throat. "Yes, well, thank you for not kicking us out of your, um, establishment." I hold on to the bat while Shonda talks about her latest class. After two minutes, she informs us she has an extracurricular meeting to attend. After she leaves, Blake recalls he has to study and departs, leaving me with just Seth.

I gently place Bat Nathanson back in the carrier and shut the tiny door. When I look up, Seth is grinning and studying me.

"What?"

"Nothing. I'm just proud of you, man."

I huff. I don't know Seth well, but he seems to treat everyone like they're his best friend.

"For having a familiar?"

"No. For bagging a vampire."

My eyebrows rise and I look away, heat flooding my face. "Um...wha...?"

"Dude, he talks to the water polo team, and they talk to me. I'm not here to blow up your gossip." I turn to see his smug face. He continues, "I'm just congratulating you. Clay's not an easy one to lock down."

I clear my throat and stare at my pet like my life depends on it. "Yes, well...we've come to a platonic lab partner agreement. No locking down, just some...fun," I murmur.

He scoffs. "Dude, an academic like you knows that familiars don't just bond to two random 'platonic lab partners.'" He uses air quotes, and I wish he was back in his mummy's tomb.

"I can't speak for Bat Nathanson. Or anyone." I push up my glasses and sip my tea. "I don't catch feelings for jocks."

"Mhm," Seth responds. He sounds as unconvinced as I do. He sips from his cup and his scrutiny makes me want to curl up in a ball. He can obviously tell that I'm crushing on Clay way harder than I ever thought possible.

"Is that why you're here? Waiting to hand off your little pet to his co-parent?"

"Exactly," I reply, swiveling my cup of tea. "We're lab partners and co-parents."

"And no feelings."

"Nope, none." I smile, managing to lie to even myself.

"All right, well, you should probably let him know that, because here he comes." Seth dashes away, and my smile falls.

When I turn around, the sight is like slow motion—Clay is walking toward me, hair perfectly coiffed as always. Not seeing him for a few days has made me miss his handsome face, and my heart won't stop racing.

"I am so sorry, Owen."

"What, why?" I ask, standing up.

"I kept you waiting. Our commute was slammed with traffic, and it took us forever to get back to campus."

"Right, you and your flying vampire friends." I swallow down a pang of jealousy while he stares into the carrier at Bat Nathanson.

"How's the baby?"

"He's good. Missed you."

"Aw, I'm glad he's all right. Did you have a good time with Papa?"

The bat mewls, and the exchange squeezes my heart. Clay is so charming, thoughtful, sweet, and domestic.

But I've made it clear time and time again that I don't date jocks. I've sabotaged any possibility of us becoming serious. It seems lab partners and co-parents are all we'll ever be, and I'm the one to blame.

My shoulders nearly sag at the thought. Before I can say more, Clay stands up straight and holds the carrier. He smiles at me, and I want to melt. "Hey, so are you free next weekend?"

"Hm?"

He rolls his shoulders and looks away. "I read that there's this new exhibit in the museum all about flying animals. I was wondering if you wanted to go with me, since I've never been."

My eyebrows scrunch. "Like...take Bat Nathanson there for a field trip?"

He chuckles. "Yeah, we could. Or just...the two of us. You and me. Going to a museum." He shyly smiles at the carrier. "We could get dinner afterwards, or something...if you want."

I don't even have time to overthink this before I yelp, "Yes!"

Clay gazes at me and nods. "Perfect. See you in class then." He holds up the carrier. "Say goodnight to Papa!"

"Squeak!" our pet responds.

I snicker. "Bye," I whisper. The pair strolls away and my heart continues to race.

Clay Cannon. *Asked me out.* I might melt in happiness.

A moment later, I look up and notice Mummy Mocha is deserted. They've closed up, but Seth stands nearby, cleaning a cup. He bounces his eyebrows at me, and I know he heard that whole exchange.

"I...uh...we..." I stammer, and Seth continues to look smug. "Just...shut up," I mutter. I power walk away while the mummy laughs at my expense.

But how can I care? I have a date with the hottest, sweetest vampire dude on campus. Now I just need to not mess this up.

FIFTEEN

CLAY

I've seen Owen excited before, like how happy he was when I flew for the first time, or how he was glowing when he got an A on a quiz in Monster Anatomy. He was ecstatic when Bat Nathanson was healed enough to take off his bandages and stretch his wings. And of course, Owen loves a blow job as much as the next guy.

But I don't think I've ever seen him as genuinely thrilled as he is right now. Owen's eyes have been sparkling since he got in my car, he's been babbling about how world-class the Creelin Natural History Museum's mammalian collection is and how excited he is to see the new bat exhibit. Now he's bouncing from foot to foot as we wait in line to enter.

Part of me hopes that his enthusiasm isn't only because we're going to the museum, but that he genuinely enjoys spending time with me. Because he keeps touching my hand, my forearm, and my bicep. He'll knock me with his shoulder as he makes a point. And all in all, I hope he simply likes touching me. If my body temperature ever changed, I'm sure that the feel of his skin would warm my heart. I'm feeding off of his excitement, wanting to get closer and closer to him the more I'm with him. I focus on the dark brown depths of his eyes, how slim and animated his fingers are, and how passionate he gets when talking about the sea creatures that are supposed to be on display.

I like watching him. I like being around him. I like his gorgeous face and his deep-dives into subjects I know nothing about. He's just so...pure. Sweet. Cute.

Sexy.

And his ass in those dark-wash jeans belongs in a museum. So I guess we're in the right place.

"I haven't seen the new exhibit yet, but I've heard all about it," Owen says, squeezing my hand. I show my phone to the werewolf at the door, and he scans our tickets.

"I've never been here. I haven't spent much time in museums," I admit. "Normally I hate old things."

"But you're willing to do this for me?"

I shrug, gesturing for him to go inside. "It's not a hardship. I enjoy spending time with you. Plus, I heard this place is great." I grin at him.

The shy smile I get in response takes my breath away.

The moment Owen and I step foot inside the museum, I understand why people all over Fangstagram recommend going here on a date.

For one, there's its location next to the Lin River. With floor-to-ceiling windows along the back wall, we have an incredible view of the water. I spy a group of phoenix shifters sitting in the cafeteria patio outside drinking white wine and enjoying the nice weather while some tiny cyclops children run in the grass. I'll definitely be taking Owen out there for lunch.

Then there's the amazing entrance exhibit. Immediately upon walking in, there are fossils of huge dinosaurs, all fascinating and educational. The rest of the museum is probably just as interesting. I'm starting to see the merit in science and ancient objects.

"What do you want to see first?" I ask.

"I wanna see the hall of birds," Owen says, reading a directional sign on the wall. "Maybe we can see one of those feather fossils, the ones that connect birds with Pteranodons, you know?"

"Because I lived through it, right?" I huff. A family of humans passes us, and some zombies head toward the sign that says, *Insect World.*

He shakes his head. "Nah. You're not that old."

I stare at him in surprise as we walk down the hall. "You turned down the chance to make a joke about how I was there with the dinosaurs."

"I'm sure you've heard enough jokes about that to last a lifetime."

"Thanks," I say, feeling warm again. "I've been sensitive about my age for, oh, twenty years now. It's hard to look like this and be as old as I really am."

"I like you just how you are," he says.

This man. He's always perfect. Something lodges inside me, a feeling I've never felt before.

I care about this man. I want to keep him. Am I falling for him?

Owen peers at me through his glasses and gives me an unreserved, crooked smile. My heart bangs in my chest.

Yeah, I'm falling for him.

He needs to be mine.

I glance around, my stomach fluttering and my knees weak. "So, are you going to be my tour guide?"

"Sure! I think we should check out the west wing first."

"Then lead the way." I follow him with a light, bouncing step, smiling at nothing and everything.

Yes, we go see the birds and the bats and the sea creatures of all kinds. The museum houses some funny, old-fashioned dioramas of stuffed animals and all sorts of skeletons. We take our time in the exhibits, looking at fossils from all over the world.

But as much as I like the educational aspects of this institution, what I'm really enjoying are the dark nooks we come to where I can steal a kiss. My favorite is the gemstone exhibit, since it's almost entirely in the dark, with dramatic lighting only illuminating the faceted stones. As Owen pauses to stare at a huge, dark red crystal of some kind, I come up behind him and wrap my arms around his waist.

Oh, how I want to feed off his warm neck. Holy monster god, the pulse of his blood is overwhelming. I run my lips along the salty skin just under his jawline. I shouldn't tease myself. Except, in response, he presses his ass subtly into my groin, and I want to moan.

I tsk into his ear. "Don't get me hard in public."

"It'd only be fair. You make me so horny all the time," he murmurs.

"I feel like we have to keep stealing time when our roommates are away to get together."

"Yeah." He sighs.

"What do you think of this plan," I say carefully, as we shuffle over to a large blue stone of some sort. "We get you some lunch at the café here, then I take you to a hotel and fuck your brains out."

Owen's eyebrows jump. He looks around and pushes his glasses up in his usual adorable way. "You know, I think I've absorbed enough museum knowledge for one afternoon. I'm good. Not even hungry. No lunch required. Haha!"

I smirk. I let him guide me by the hand to the nearest exit.

We're on the same page for the second part of this date. *Yuss.*

Twenty minutes later, we're pulling into a decent hotel nearby, the kind where parents of students stay when they're in town to visit. While I don't mind quick sex in a car or a custodian's closet, with Owen, I want it to be more special. I want to take my time. I also want to make sure we have the proper space so I'm not bumping into the steering wheel—done that—or a mop bucket —done that too. And Yuki might be sick of me kicking him out.

After I get the keycard for our rental, I raise an eyebrow. "I really want to throw you over my shoulder and fly you up to the room."

Owen shivers. "Will that be faster? I think the room's right there." He points two doors down.

"Oh, right. Well, next time."

He laughs nervously as he follows me to the door.

"Hey," I say, studying his face and lifting his chin up with my finger. "If you don't want to do this, we don't have to."

"Oh my monster god, vamp," Owen says. "I'm dying here. Stop stalling." He pauses. "Unless you don't want to."

I step closer to him. "I very much want to."

Using the keycard, I open the door and step inside the generic but clean hotel room. The moment he's inside and the door shuts behind him, I put my mouth on his. He kisses me back ravenously, all trepidation gone in an instant. His back's to the door, and one of my legs is between his as I cage him in with my arms on either side of his head. Then I grip his chin with one hand.

"How do you want to do this?" I pant between kisses. My cock is hard in my jeans, my nerve endings are tingling, and I shiver in pleasurable anticipation.

"You, inside me," he pants back, clawing at my back.

"Fine with me. I'm vers, so your wish is my command. What about a condom?" I ask. "I haven't been with anyone since we've been hooking up, but I'll use one if it makes you feel better or if you don't want a mess."

"No condom," he whispers.

Stepping back, I reach in my pockets and throw some packets of lube and a few condoms on the bed. "If you change your mind, I brought some."

"More than one?"

I shrug. "Vampires have stamina."

"Especially *jock* vampires," he mutters. He kisses me and takes a step back, angling his head toward the bathroom and kicking off his shoes. "Give me a moment, yeah?"

"Go ahead." I wave him off, even though I don't want him to go anywhere without me. But even I can let him take care of bottom preparations in private.

While Owen preps, I pace, messing with the lights until I think they're sexy enough. I take off my shoes, and then I consider whether I should just strip, or let him do it.

I clear my throat and stare at myself in the small mirror above the TV. I'm blinking rapidly and my muscles are quivering.

Why am I so nervous? *Get it together, Cannon.*

It's not like this is the first time I've had sex. I shove my hands in my pockets. Twenty-plus years in a twenty-year-old body is a lot of experience.

But with Owen, things feel different. Special. Yes, I'm horny and so is he, but it feels like more than that. We really *like* each other—at least, I really like him, and I think he feels the same way. Or maybe I hope he does. He says he does. It's not so much that everything feels new or anything cheesy like that, but being with him feels *right*. Some missing part of me clicks into place when he's around. He's smart, caring, and strong in the ways I'm not. I like to think that I do something for him, too.

The toilet flushes, the faucet runs and turns off, and then Owen steps out of the bathroom. My fangs descend.

Holy fuck.

On my list of things I like about Owen that I recited in my head just now, I forgot to mention that he's absolutely the sexiest man I could ever ask for, period. Exactly my type. He's not tall or short, not big or small, just...perfect.

And he looks even better right now. His dark hair's mussed. His lips are swollen from our kisses. His eyes are half-lidded with desire. There's a very clear outline of his cock in the front of his jeans.

I want him.

He pushes up his glasses, bites his lip, and before he can open his mouth, I vampire-zoom over to him and pick his ass up so he has no choice but to wrap his legs around my waist.

"You good?" I ask.

"Yep," he says, and threads his hands into my hair, pulling me close for a kiss.

I pull back. "Careful of the fangs."

"Yeah, yeah, I know."

"Monster god, you're sexy," I whisper, palming his ass.

Before he can respond, I kiss him and walk us toward the bed. I let our tongues tangle, but I'm cautious not to accidentally make him bleed—although that would be extremely yummy.

When my knees hit the bed, I fall forward, so he drops on his back, and I go with him, settling between his legs and framing his face with my elbows as I hover over him. "I love your glasses, but want to take them off?"

Owen nods, and he looks adorable. I like that he lets me do things for him sometimes. It makes me feel competent. I know it's just taking off his glasses, but so many people don't trust me with anything. The fact that he lets me do this makes me feel like I'm caring for him, even in a simple way.

Using both hands so they don't snag on his ears, I gingerly remove his glasses and place them on the bedside table. I reach behind my head and yank my own shirt off, and I hear a sharp intake of breath from him. So I might flex my abs. Maybe.

Grinning down at him, I watch him take me in. It's flattering that he likes my body. But this is terribly one-sided.

"Get naked," I order.

"Make me, Cannon," he sasses back. I didn't know he had that in him, and I like it.

I raise an eyebrow. "I could just rip them off." I show him one of my nails, allowing it to be razor-sharp with my vampire powers.

He gazes at my nail and licks his lips. "How about the normal way this time?" Owen asks. I lower my nail. Still, I can sense his desire—the thrum of his blood and the hitch in his breath. Sometime, I'll have to shred his clothes, just to let him know how much I want him. But I'll do it with clothes he doesn't mind losing, on a day when he won't have to do a naked walk of shame afterward.

"Deal." Tugging at the hem of his T-shirt, he helps me get his top off and then I go back over him again.

This is better. Skin to skin. My cold skin against his hot, velvety skin makes everything feel like it's the right temperature. Not too cool or too warm.

"Ugh, you feel so *good*," he mutters, as he squeezes my shoulders. I snake a hand down to the front of his pants, rubbing his hard length with my palm, careful not to be too rough or to press his zipper into him.

I lean down and kiss and lick my way along his torso. I'd

bite him too, but that's too dangerous. So I keep everything light.

As I'm doing that, he runs his nails along my scalp.

"Keep doing that," I say, breathlessly. "I love it."

He obliges, running those perfect fingers through my hair. Next, I undo his jeans and hook my thumbs in his underwear. Between the two of us, we take all of his clothing off, so he's now naked under me.

"Every time I see you naked, I think how lucky I am to get to touch you," I whisper. "You're so fucking sexy."

Heat infuses his cheeks. "Seriously? I'm not—"

He's going to say something self-deprecating. I cut him off. "I really dig your look, okay? Please, don't say anything negative, Bhat."

Owen nods. "Okay."

Descending back down on him, I run my hands up the inside of his legs, along his calves and thighs, and when I get to his cock, I run the back of my index finger up the underside.

I know he wants more. I want more. But I also want to tease him a bit before we go further. So I open my mouth and take his tip inside, suckling gently.

He hisses. "Fuck, I love your mouth."

Bobbing up and down on his cock, I use my tongue to play with the area under the head—I should know the name, we're in anatomy class together. Frenulum, maybe?

All I know is that it feels good.

Owen seems to agree, judging by how his heartbeat is racing and he's leaking precum. As I suck him, I fumble for one of those packets of lube I threw on the bed earlier, but it's just out of reach.

I pop off of him. "Hang on," I say, and wink, nuzzling his hipbone. Might as well take off my clothes, too. I shove off my jeans, underwear, and socks, and stroke my cock a few times, while Owen watches me from the bed, his hand on his own cock.

I need to be inside him. I *have* to have him. I find one of the packets, rip it, and pour liquid on my fingers as I come back up on the bed.

"Sorry this is cold," I say. "Both my fingers and the lube."

"It's fine," Owen says. He jumps a little as my fingers find his entrance and I spread the fluid.

Taking my time, I circle his hole, adding more lube and penetrating him with one finger. While I'm probably coordinated enough to suck his cock at the same time, I like watching the expressions on his face, and I don't want to miss the way he squeezes his eyes shut and then opens them in pleasure when that initial burn eases. More lube is always good, so I drizzle more and add a second finger, taking my time to open him up. He sucks in a hard breath when I graze his prostate, and I grin.

"How're you doing, sexy?" I ask.

"Good. Very good."

I raise an eyebrow. "I can do better than that, I think."

"I just want you inside me," he whines.

"In a minute." I don't want to hurt him, even though that initial fullness of a dick in your ass always stings no matter how much a dude preps. And he just feels so warm and tight; I like playing with him.

But when he's no longer tense and starts begging, "Clay, please, now," I relent.

"On your knees?" I ask. "Is that how you want it?"

"Yes, fuck, please, yes." Owen flips onto his hands and knees, and I take a moment to admire him.

Dark brown skin. That gorgeous ass. The dark hair on his legs. His strong back. His masculine scent. His heat.

He's mine.

Coming up behind him, I kiss the back of his neck. I pour

the rest of the lube on my cock and rub it, making a total mess. But I don't care—sex is messy, but sheets can be washed.

Holding my dick against his hole, I use my hips to gradually press in.

He resists me at first, and I'm forced out so I have to try it again. But this time I pop in up to the head, then slowly keep going in as he groans in pleasure.

"Oh monster god," I whisper, my hands on his hips. "You're so tight...and hot...and...feel so good."

"Nrgh," he replies, which makes me smile.

Making my way inside him, I finally seat myself entirely in his ass, with my pelvis against his ass cheeks.

I suck on his neck, wanting to bite, but knowing this will have to do. And I hold, letting him adjust. Letting his body accept me.

Finally, he nods, and I do an experimental pull out and thrust in, just a little bit.

He grunts.

"You good?" I ask.

He nods.

"Words, Owen. Are you okay?"

"So fucking okay."

I grin against his neck and reach around for his cock, which has flagged.

Now I start to fuck him, using the lube still on my fingers to stroke his cock at the same time I thrust in and pull out. At the beginning, I do small movements, not wanting to hurt him, but once I know he's into it—when he starts shoving his ass back onto me—I go faster and harder, adjusting the angle until—*there*—I'm nudging his prostate.

And now I let myself enjoy the ride.

I'm losing myself in his hot body. In the rhythm of our

movements. In how he meets me thrust for thrust. In how perfectly we fit together.

In how his blood sings under my fingers. How my cock is drowning in pleasure in his body. How hard he is, and how his balls are drawing up tight to his body. How we smell like sweat and sex and salt and—okay, only I can smell this—the sharp tang of blood.

I could back off and keep edging him, but I think we both want to come.

"You close?" I murmur.

"Yeah, so close."

Changing the angle, I find one that makes him moan loudly. I stroke his cock, focusing on the tip and the underside, and his body tightens up as he's in that moment before he's going to come. That pause before he shatters.

With a groan, he starts coming, his hot release all over my hand as I fuck him through it.

Then a few more thrusts of my own in what is surely his oversensitive body, and I'm taking my own shattering leap.

It's better than scoring a goal.

It's better than flying.

It's better than anything—the waves of pleasure hit me over and over again as I fuck into him, shoving myself inside him deep and staying there through all of the pulsing. My mind is clear, my body's satisfied, and my heart...it's happy.

I hold him as both of us pant like we've run a race.

Owen turns his face over his shoulder, and I kiss him savagely. In my enthusiasm, I accidentally nick his lip, rendering a slight trace of blood on his mouth.

"Sorry," I whisper, wanting to lick it.

"Nothing to be sorry about," he says, sucking on his lip so that it stops.

With Owen, the more I have him, the more I want him. I think this feeling's never going to stop.

After a few moments, I pull out and give him another kiss, then go to the bathroom to clean up.

I can only dwell on one thought: I want to do that again as soon as he's ready.

When I get back to bed with a warm washcloth to clean him off, I curl up behind him, holding him to me.

"That was..." he whispers.

"Yeah. It was."

SIXTEEN

OWEN

I haven't been this happy in years. When I chose to transfer to Creepin U, a bonafide monster school, I had goals in mind. I wanted to do monster-focused pre-med, but deep down, I actually wanted to hook up with monsters. My parents thought it was an awful idea, but the results speak for themselves: I'm passing Monster Anatomy class with flying colors.

Oh, and I'm dating Clay. My heart wants to take off like a firework.

This hot vampire jock is so sweet and gentlemanly. When I'm with him, he lavishes attention on me. It's like no one else exists. I adore his fangs and tight body, but the moments when we're just taking care of BN make him just as attractive. He's a great dad to our little guy. Of course, the thrilling anal sex is a fun bonus, too.

We've gone out twice, and slept together each time. My heart grows and grows, and a small part of me wants to tell the world he's mine. Another part of me is afraid of how my parents will react when they find out I'm in a budding relationship with a fanged flying dude. You would think brown folks in America would be more accepting of people who are different, but unfortunately, conservatism is oftentimes illogical.

I've made it clear to Clay that during class we have to be strictly platonic. But I already informed him that, based on how we've nailed our projects and quizzes so far, the lowest we can get is a C, and that's assuming we fail the final. So in short, we're coasting for the rest of the semester. Anatomy class may be essentially over, but I have no intention of letting Clay go.

I'm waiting for him in the corner of Mummy Mocha while patrons mull about. He claims he has a surprise for me since we did so well on our recent anatomy project on the cremasteric reflex. I sip my coffee and check under the towel of the pet carrier on the table. The ambient noise doesn't appear to be bothering Bat Nathanson. I'm handing him off for the week, but I can't imagine not caring for my little pet bat—yet another reason why Clay and I should be together.

But are we official boyfriends? I scroll through my tablet, reading several articles about modern vampire anthropology. Anatomy class didn't touch upon the act of feeding off of a regular human. Every article I've read details that sucking blood is such an intimate process. Like sex, consent is mandatory—in fact, according to hundreds of anecdotes, feeding often occurs during or after sex with the partner they care for the most.

I shut off my tablet and frown at my coffee cup. Maybe it's too soon? We only started doing anal two weeks ago. We haven't discussed labels. The other—overthinking, paranoid—part of my brain postulates that Clay doesn't want me long term, hence his forbearance from biting me. We've been intimate for weeks now, surely he would have at least broached the topic, right?

I tap my cup and sigh. My insecurities are flaring up.

A few moments later, when I spot my guy strolling in, all my fear fades away. His smile is dazzling, and my heart continues to fall for him.

"Hey, you," he says. He steals a kiss with superhuman speed, and I'll never get over his casual displays of affection.

I can't keep a giggle from slipping out of my mouth. "Clay. What's up?"

"I brought you a surprise." He holds up his hand and I peer at the towel-wrapped object.

"Usually I detest unknown variables." I stroke his arm. "But since you're good-looking, I'll allow it."

He snickers and opens the towel. "Well, it's not really a gift for you. But, um..."

I take in the object—it's a tiny piece of pink fabric, and in dark marker, it reads *Bat Nathanson*.

My smile falls. "Is this...?"

Clay shrugs. "Yuki helped me crochet it. I figured since he's no ordinary bat, we could put this little bandana on him. Let the whole world know who he is, kind of like a dog tag."

My heart bounces around my chest like a ping pong. "You... made this for our baby?"

"Of course." He beams and flashes his fangs. "Do you like it?"

"Oh, it's splendiferous!" I gush, holding up the small fabric. "You should put it on him tonight when he's awake. Bat Nathanson is snoring right now."

"That's fair." Clay pockets the crocheted bandana and pulls the carrier closer to him. He's so thoughtful that I can't take it. So, I lean in and hug him.

"You're the best," I whisper. *The best thing I've ever let into my life.* I don't say those last words, but they're throbbing in my soul.

"You flatter me, Bhat," he replies, squeezing me tightly.

"Aww!" We pull apart at the sound of an unfamiliar voice.

The two people standing near us holding coffee look vaguely familiar, but...

"I'm sorry, but you two are too cute," the female remarks.

Clay looks wildly at them, then at me, then back at them.

"Um..." he says. I gaze at the duo and notice their skin has a bluish pallor.

"Bro, I didn't know you had a feeder," the male says.

They're vampires! Of course, they were part of the Vampire Gliding Enthusiasts I saw that one time.

I shake my head as the words finally permeate my consciousness. "Feeder?" I whisper.

Clay continues to say nothing. "And he's cute," the girl says. "We totally have feeder boyfriends and girlfriends who attend some of our field trips. They're our biggest supporters." She smiles and looks up. "And of course, they keep our energy up. Don't go on a trip without your blood-filled buddy, we always say. Ha!"

They laugh. "How rude of us to not invite your boy, Clay." The guy exchanges a knowing glance with the girl. "Had we known you had a human of your own, we would have gladly made room for him on our trips."

"He's...not my human," Clay replies.

"And I have never fed anyone." My face feels numb, and I stand up abruptly. I ignore their confused looks and hike up my backpack. "I gotta run."

"You do?" Clay asks.

"We're off, too," the girl vampire says. "We just wanted to say hi."

"I have to, um, call my mom," I mumble.

"Right this second?" I don't miss the concern in Clay's eyes, but I really can't be here right now.

"Um, yeah. Bye." I shake my head at the ground and power walk out of there, leaving the vampires behind. My body is on autopilot as I march to my room. I don't dare look at my phone as I launch myself onto my bed and shut my eyes. I think a nap is in order.

He's not my human. Clay's words won't stop echoing through my brain until I fall asleep. Maybe when I wake up, I'll be worthy of being Clay's feeder, but I doubt it.

THE NEXT MORNING, Anatomy class is fascinating. Well, not actually, but I listen and watch Octavia with stalwart scrutiny, anything to ignore Clay's prying eyes next to me. I take notes and say nothing to him even though we're already passing the class with flying colors.

It's immature to feel so hurt, but tell that to my heart. Clay doesn't owe me any sex or blood-sucking, and I have to accept that.

When I sense the lecture is almost over, I don't wait for Octavia to stop talking before I haul ass out of there. Of course, I don't make it far before Clay catches up to me—friggin' vampire super-speed.

"Owen, would you wait up?"

I barge through the doors without stopping. The warm spring air greets my cheeks and I fixate on the blooming trees. "I'm kinda busy."

"With what?"

"Studies, and uh, books." I don't slow down. We walk past three witches playing hackey sack. The campus is abuzz with stress-free happiness, and I wish I could join them.

"You didn't answer my texts."

"Oops, sorry," I say with a flat tone.

"Would you stop for a second please?" He grabs my arm, and I have no choice but to stop. I turn around and notice we're near the very busy parking lot.

"What is it?" I ask, not even looking at his face.

"Are you...are you angry at me?"

The hurt look on his face clenches my soul, but I need to be strong. I bite my lip and look away. "Why would I be angry?"

"Is it because I said you weren't my human feeder?"

I hike up my backpack and look at the sky. "Why would that make me upset? It's true."

"Owen." He touches my shoulders and I have no choice but to gaze into his precious eyes. "You know you mean more to me than being some random human."

The fight in me deflates; for weeks now, Clay Cannon has been my ultimate weakness. "Do you...need a feeder?"

He lets go and rolls his neck. "We don't *need* them, per se."

"Is that why I'm not worthy enough for you to feed on me when we have sex?"

His eyes blow wide; it would be almost comical if we weren't both upset.

"Owen, you—"

The sounds of two car doors closing startles us both.

"Yoohoo! Owen!" Hearing that voice, the blood drains from my face so fast I almost faint. Before I can react, someone is gripping me tightly. I exchange a glance with Clay, but he's frozen in shock as well.

"Mom! Dad!" I yelp, as my parents crowd me.

SEVENTEEN

CLAY

The two people who ambushed us are seriously invading our personal space, but my protective instincts dissolve the second I learn they're Owen's parents.

Owen's mouth flies open and his fingers touch his parted lips. "What are you doing here?"

"Well, that's a fine way to greet your mother," his father says, and I can't tell if he's being stern or joking. He's the same height as Owen, although a little heavier, and wearing black slacks and a dark-blue plaid dress shirt. His brown hair's thinner than Owen's, but they have the same eye shape and color, and their noses are identical. If Owen grows up to look like him, he'll be a very handsome man.

"We wanted to surprise you," his mother says. She's shorter than Owen and his father, and is wearing a bright pink long-sleeved blouse over a long blue skirt that reaches to her ankles. Her dark hair is pinned back in a complicated bun.

Judging by the dazed look on Owen's face, mission accomplished on the surprise plan.

But the fact that he has his parents here is important. At

least they care enough to visit and be a part of his world. I'd give anything for my parents to give a shit about what I'm doing. He's lucky to have them in his life.

Owen's eyes are still bulging at being caught unaware, but he's starting to recover. "Well, hey, then. It's good to see both of you." And he gives them each a hug.

That simple gesture makes my chest ache for things I haven't had in a long time. *If only I had a family...*

Then they all turn and face me.

I may be in my fourth decade of life, but I still suppress a wince when I learn someone's parents are around. It's like I'm a teenager and a bad influence on their son. Guess I still feel like I'll be judged and found wanting. I probably should've gone to therapy about that instinct a long time ago, but I thought that ghost had vanished.

Owen catches my eyes, trying to communicate *something* to me, but I'm not sure what. "This is Clay. He and I are...lab partners. In the anatomy class we just had."

Lab partners.

"We finally get to meet a friend of Owen's. You'll have to join us for lunch," his father says.

I freeze.

How do I play this? Is Owen out to his parents? Am I a friend or a boyfriend? Can I sit next to him and hold his hand, or should I pretend like all my feelings for him are platonic? Are we just lab partners, like Owen said?

Studying Owen's face again, I can't get a read on what he wants me to do, so I might as well stay quiet and bow out.

I start to shake my head, but his mother steps forward. "We insist that you come."

"I'm really not hungry," I say, glancing around. "If I get hungry later, I can just go to the cafeteria."

"Don't be silly, you're a young college man. You must be sick of the monster-themed food here. We're happy to treat you," his mom says.

"It's not a question of funds..." I start, then get a glimpse of Owen's face. His lips are pinched, and he keeps running his hands through his hair. I open my eyes wide. *What do I do?*

He shrugs.

I smile. "Okay, then. I'm happy to join in. Thanks for the invite."

I'm sure this meal will be no big deal.

We pile into their car and Owen's dad drives us to downtown Creelin while my brain races to figure out how to act. My heart sinks as they pull up to a restaurant that caters to humans. No blood on the menu, that's for sure. *Maybe I can get like a really rare steak?*

We file into the restaurant, and I take in the scent of curry and peppers. "So, young man, how are you handling being at... *such* a university?" his mother asks me.

Do they not realize I'm a vampire? I suppose if my fangs aren't descended and you don't look too hard at my coloring, I can pass for human.

Oh, shit. What do his parents think about monsters? Is that the problem?

Ugh. Even after decades of dealing with micro-aggressions and blatant anti-monster rhetoric, I still need a moment to figure out how to respond. I don't want to pretend that what she's doing is right, but I also don't want to ruin things with Owen.

We're shown to our seats, and I'm handed a menu where, yes, nothing on there is anything I'd be able to eat.

I pretend to sip my water. "Well, I'm on the water polo team, so that was much of my focus last semester."

"I was meaning more, if you were having any issues with the...*other* students," she says. Her face screams discomfort.

"Mom!" Owen whines.

"What? It's normal for me to find out how other humans cope at a school such as yours."

With how Owen's hands are fidgeting, though, I know he's not comfortable having me along. Does he get really anxious? I've seen him on edge with classwork and the general stress of school. But right now, he seems more nervous than I've observed him in the past. The last thing I want is for him to have a panic attack. I don't know how to answer her question without giving myself away, so I need to get out of here.

"No issues," I say. I rise from my chair. "Excuse me. I'm just going to go wash my hands."

Before anyone says anything else, I hurry to the restroom. Once inside, I stare at my reflection in the mirror.

What do I do? What the fuck do I do? I don't want to do anything to hurt Owen's relationship with his parents. Or to hurt him.

I splash water on my face and hands and dry them with a towel. Might as well return to the most awkward lunch in history.

But as I make my way back, my vampire super-hearing picks up their conversation. I'm not at the dining room yet, but it's easy for me to hear Owen's mom from behind the partition. "Beta, we cannot continue to fund a lifestyle so...irresponsible."

"*Irresponsible?*" he hisses. It's barely above a whisper. His heartbeat picks up, and he's trying to quell his anxiety, I can hear it. "All I've ever done is be responsible. I'm working to become a doctor at your behest, for crying out loud."

Owen's only becoming a doctor because of them?

"At a *monster* university," his mom replies. My throat constricts, and I stare at the floor as I continue to eavesdrop. "Son, you are not like them. Their bodies and lifestyles are different. Your father and I fear for your safety every moment of every day. What kind of future can you establish being surrounded by people who shift into wolves and tentacle creatures?"

"Mom—" Owen says.

"Your life experience will never be like theirs. Being at this school is, at best, ineffective. And at worst, it's dangerous. Some of the students drink blood!"

"Mom, please," Owen says.

"Don't interrupt your mother," his dad replies.

"Imagine if a vampire got particularly hungry one night and wanted to drink from your arteries. How could you defend yourself against that? Monsters can be friendly among themselves, but vampire-types only want to eat humans." His mom's voice is low, but also fierce.

"Mom," Owen replies. My first instinct is to dash in there and defend Owen from his folks. I want to hold him and kiss the panic away.

But my second instinct makes more sense: Owen's parents aren't lying. At best, my life as a vampire is wildly different from Owen's. And at worst, my hunger for blood makes me a liability to his health and wellness.

"*You're dangerous.*" My own parents' words echo through my mind all these decades later.

I am *going* to hurt Owen. I've been kidding myself to think that this thing between him and me could work out long term. I'm a novelty, and a dangerous one at that. It's better for him if I just stay away.

A devastating rock forms in my gut. I know what I have to do. Squaring my shoulders, I let my fangs descend and stride past the partition.

When I sit down, I lean back in my chair like I'm a haughty asshole. With a wicked grin on my lips, I throw an arm around Owen's shoulders. "I don't know why I bother looking in a mirror. I can't see myself!" I cackle obnoxiously, and now I have the whole Bhat family's attention.

"What?" Owen's mom asks. She shares a horrified look with her husband.

"It comes with the territory of being a bloodsucker." I snort, making sure she can see all my teeth. "You didn't know I'm a vampire?"

It's a long five seconds as the Bhat family stares at me in stunned silence.

"Uh...certainly not," his father says, and Owen's face crumples.

I know it may hurt, but this is good for him. This is what he needs.

I give them both my most lascivious grin. "Your son and I are in Monster Anatomy together, and boy, let me tell you how hard it's been to not suck on Owen's veins this whole time." I dramatically gesture my hands like I'm biting into an invisible hot dog. "There's nothing like waking up and chugging on some plasma and hemoglobin from a human, any human at all. That's all we vampires want, and it's not like anyone has garlic and pepper spray. Ha! That wouldn't even work on my kind. Holy water doesn't do anything. Nothing can stop me from munching on a nice, full artery!"

Owen's parents fidget and exchange fearful glances with each other. *Mission accomplished.*

Owen hasn't spoken, wide eyes frozen behind his glasses. I hate doing this to him, but it's for his own good.

I lean forward and pick up the menu. "So, Bhat fam, what are we ordering for appetizers? Hopefully some AB positive cocktails?"

This snaps them out of it. Mr. Bhat shakes his head while Mrs. Bhat says, "No. No, I won't have this. I'm afraid we've made a mistake. We cannot have a monster spending time with our son."

"Wait, what?" Owen mutters, shaking his head.

I stand up, giving them a little bow. "That's quite all right. Just enjoy your meal and don't think of me sinking my fangs into your son's jugular. He might be safer going to a human-only med school."

Then, I spin on my heel and stride slowly and with dignity, out of the restaurant. I take ten steps before I shatter, my shoulders sagging as I lean against a lamppost.

Before, I can take off at vampire super-speed back to campus, I hear footsteps behind me.

"Clay, wait!"

I stop on the sidewalk outside the restaurant, with my back to him. "What is it, Owen?" I say in a raspy tone.

"What were you doing back there? How could you just lie to my parents like that, acting like some...some uncontrollable bloodsucker?" I can hear how desperate and broken he is. "What's gotten into you?"

Pinching my nose, I try not to inhale his sweet scent.

This is better for him. It's more important that he be safe.

I turn around and face Owen, my legs planted wide. I make myself tower over him. "None of that was a lie."

"What?" Owen's voice is incredulous. He rubs his eyebrow and frowns.

"I'm a vampire." I put a hand on my hip.

"Okay? I know, and?" he snaps.

Leaning in closer, I say, "I drink blood."

Owen glares at me. "I know that too."

Please understand. This is for your own good. "I want to drink *your* blood. That makes me dangerous to you."

"What? But you're not danger—"

"Yes, I am," I hiss. "You can't tell what's going on inside my head. I'm no good for you. Just forget about me, Owen. Take good care of Bat Nathanson and go on and live a happy life. Heed your parents' advice, attend a human medical school, and have the career you were always meant to have, far away from my kind."

Owen opens his mouth to say something, but I don't want to hear his arguments. Nothing he could say could change my mind. This is the right thing to do. He needs to not throw his life away, which is what he'd be doing spending time with me.

With that, I run off in a blur.

CHAPTER

EIGHTEEN

OWEN

Well, this is misery. I'm expected to be a content, studious, demure son while my parents drive me all over the town. I'm supposed to act accordingly as my folks take me to Wraithmart to buy bedsheets and underwear. I have to be all smiles as they insist on buying me groceries at Claws-Co. And I even need to be friendly with my folks while we have dinner at Bengal Palace, the only Indian restaurant within a one-hour radius. Admittedly, it was entertaining seeing them act uncomfortable with the owner of the last place, a werecat Bengal tiger shifter.

But my heart feels torn to shreds. My super-hot kind-of-boyfriend probably broke up with me. Does it count if you were only ever lab partners who occasionally fucked? And also you're raising a small woodland creature together? Okay, when I think about it like that, it's somehow gayer and more domestic.

I thought that Clay cared about me, that what we had was something special. Instead, he goes full Morbius, full Dracula, full whatever-bloodsucker I'm supposed to be scared of, and terrifies my parents.

He doesn't even want to see Bat Nathanson anymore.

"See you tomorrow," I say as I tap on the car window. It's a warm spring night, and I'm done saying goodbye to my parents. Dad helped me carry the groceries up ten minutes ago. My roommate, Michael, didn't even acknowledge my existence, gazing at his computer screen as usual. I finished walking Dad down the stairs, we agreed to meet for brunch tomorrow, and now I'm waving them goodbye.

I'm their good son, as usual. They don't want me to work with or learn about monsters, and I guess that's what they'll get. I sigh and gaze up at the full moon. *I wish Clay was back in my arms.*

My phone buzzes and I whip it out of my pocket. "Hello?"

"Dude, get up here!"

Michael sounds panicked, and my brow furrows. I was just in our room five seconds ago.

"Wha...what?"

"It'sgoingcrazyandIcan'tstopit!"

"Michael, slow down." I scan my key card to get in and dash up the stairs. "What are you saying?"

He hangs up and my pulse races. I open my room door to chaos—Bat Nathanson's terrarium is on the floor.

And so is Michael. He's hiding behind his chair and wields his notebook like a shield.

"Owen, get IN HERE!"

"What is happening—woah!" I duck and dodge on instinct as a blur flies for my head.

"Your little pet rodent knocked over his box thing!"

What? "It's a terrarium—woah!" I dodge again at the dark foreign object spinning in the air.

"I don't care, just contain your pet THING!"

I try to track it with my gaze. "Bat?" I ask.

It screeches, and Michael howls. He swipes at the air fecklessly, and I move between them—but whom I'm protecting, I'm not sure.

This can't be. "Bat Nathanson?" I ask again.

"Yes, it's your sky puppy!" Michael shouts and cowers even further. "Tell it to stop!"

How is this happening? BN can't fly! *Unless...*

I gape at my poor, panicking roommate as the black fuzz flaps around.

I clear my throat and hold out my hands. In my sternest voice, I announce, "Bat No-Middle-Name Nathanson, you come down here, *right* now!"

The flapping sounds stop and the fuzz lands on my palms. *Success!*

"Get that thing out of here!" Michael whines.

I frown at him, then look back at my hands. Bat Nathanson simply licks his wing. "We're leaving," I say. I take a brief moment to pick up the pink scarf from the floor. I place my familiar on the desk and gently wrap the fabric around his neck. *Clay crafted this with love, and he deserves to be here for this occasion.*

"You made a mess and scared my poor roommate," I say in a chastising voice.

"I wasn't *that* scared," Michael mutters.

I cradle BN. "You knocked over your little house." I look down at the tipped-over terrarium on the floor with the latch open. "Why'd you do that, little buddy, huh?"

"Squeak!" he replies.

"I didn't know you could—woah!" The moment I open the door, he flies off. "Wait for your papa!"

I cringe at the thought of all my dorm neighbors hearing those words come out of my mouth. All the while, I dash down the stairs, following my familiar. I'm so proud he can fly now, but at the same time, I want him to slow down.

He spins around the front door, and I open it, allowing him to fly off. Is he leaving me? Suddenly, my chest hurts, and I feel dizzy. I keep following him, even though my limbs are shaking. When he gets to a nearby bench, he gradually lands. I reach him and lean my hands on my thighs as I try to catch my breath. "What are you—*hey!*"

He takes off again, and I have no choice but to follow. "Bat Nathanson, you slow down this instant!" He ignores me as I dash across campus. In a day filled with highs and lows, this takes the cake. My familiar can fly, and now he won't stop! I don't know whether to laugh or cry.

After a few minutes, he slows down and lands on a sign on the other side of campus. It's dark, but with the lamplights, I can read *Creelin Athletics Center. Huh.* I've only been here a couple of times, all to watch water polo. Maybe if I spent more time exercising here, I wouldn't be gasping for air at this moment.

"Please...please stop," I rasp, nearly wheezing. I wipe my brow and lean on a nearby trash can. *I look awful, but I don't really care who sees me right now.*

"Owen?"

I retract that previous statement. Clay, of all people, walks out the Athletics Center doors, holding a black gym bag. His hair is all wet, and he looks delicious as ever. The past few hours of being apart haven't quelled my attraction to him. Meanwhile, I probably look like the before picture for a deodorant commercial.

"Clay...you...I, uh..." I gasp and try to regain some semblance of composure.

"Are you okay? Are you asthmatic or something? Should I call the nurse?" He touches my shoulder and it's sweet.

"No, I, uh..." I gulp in air and lick my lips. Then I stand up straight and breathe out slowly. "I ran here."

"What? Why?"

"Because...because..." Our familiar lands on my head, and I point to it, not even looking up. "Because of this," I say.

"Bat Nathanson!" Clay reaches for him. "My baby, Daddy missed you," he coos.

I smile seeing him go back into loving co-parent mode. "Apparently he missed you, too."

Clay holds him up and our pet licks him. Clay laughs, and I nearly melt at how cute it is.

Then I recall his words from earlier, and my smile falls. "I thought you were, um...done with us."

Clay looks at me, and even in the lamplight, the hurt and shock on his face is undeniable.

Before he can say a word, however, Bat Nathanson squeaks. A moment later, he takes to the skies, up and up. His silhouette is clear in the moonlight, and he flies off, far, far from our reach. If Clay could jump off a tree, he might be able to catch up, but I think we both know our little guy is happy to be free, soaring among the stars.

Bat Nathanson is gone, nothing but a fleck in the dark sky. The thought of that has my heart clenching. I move closer to Clay on instinct, desperate to hold on to the only other person who understands my emotions right now. It figures that a weirdo like me would have empty nest syndrome at the ripe old age of twenty-one.

"Wow," Clay murmurs.

"I know," I rasp.

"We did it," he adds. "We successfully rehabilitated Bat Nathanson."

"Yup. Now he's a free bird, er, bat."

After a beat, Clay and I look at each other; he has his arm wrapped around my shoulder, and I gaze at his lips. Then, I pull away from him, remembering that we are not boyfriends, we never were.

"Right, well." I clear my throat and square my shoulders. "Now that that's settled, we're done here. See you in class, Mr. Cannon." I turn and try not to let my next words choke my soul. "You no longer have to pretend to enjoy hanging out with a loser human like me."

I don't take two steps before I hear him ask, "Is that what you think?"

I freeze, and a minuscule kindling of hope flares in my chest. I refuse to turn around, but stand still in the darkness. I need Clay to make this move.

I sniff. "What else should I think? After today, what you said...?"

"Owen, look at me." He touches my shoulder, and I have no choice but to turn around. "I'm sorry if I hurt you earlier, but it's not because I don't want to be with you."

"Wha...what?" He rubs my shoulders, and I push up my glasses. My eyes threaten to burn with tears—Bat Nathanson is gone, and now Clay might want me? "But you said—"

"I said it's dangerous to be near a bloodsucker like me. I said you should stay away, but it certainly isn't because I don't want to date you or be your boyfriend or anything like that."

My head goes light at the B-word. *Clay wants me?* "But you... never even considered making me your feeder."

"Yeah, because it's dangerous to be near me!" He huffs a sad laugh and looks up while rubbing my shoulders. "Oh my monster god, Owen, I've wanted to feed off of you since the day we met!"

My eyebrows jump. That can't be right. "This whole time? Why didn't you tell me?"

He bristles. "Well gee, it's not like you had a 'no dating

jocks' rule. Why would I want to put my heart on the line only for a handsome guy like you to break it?"

"What...me...break...what?"

He cards his fingers through my hair. "Owen Bhat, there isn't anything about you I don't desire. Familiar or no familiar, I want you."

Sparks cascade down my spine starting from where his fingers touch my scalp. I want so badly to bury myself in his muscly body, but we're not in the clear yet. "But earlier you said I should go to a human school and stay away."

He sighs and gently leads me to a bench. As we sit in the dark, he stares at his shoes. It's evident that he's winding up to say something important. "My...parents kicked me out after I turned."

My jaw drops. "*What?*" I whisper.

"Yeah," he mutters. He sighs and wipes his face. "They said I was dangerous. That I had fangs, and I would feast on them or their neighbors. To be fair, I broke into blood banks and sucked on raw meat for like a year, but I *never* hurt a human." He shakes his head. "But my parents couldn't get over my blood thirst. So I left."

My heart aches for him, so I rub his back. This explains quite a bit. "Clay..."

"I'm fortunate I had saved enough funds to get me by. I took a bunch of odd jobs, any job at all. Then the OME recommended I go back to school, so I did. And now look at me: I'm a forty-year-old fuck-up who doesn't know what he wants in life, and my parents don't want me."

I bite my lip. "You aren't a fuck-up. I'm sorry that happened to you."

He nods. His voice is raspy as he continues, "Being with your folks, it was like witnessing that all over again." He gazes into my eyes, and the hurt on his face is undeniable. "Owen, I refuse to be the wedge between you and your parents, I won't."

"Clay, baby." I rub his hand on his lap. "You won't, I swear. I will handle my parents." I bring his hand to my mouth and kiss it. His skin is cold, but to me, he's always been the perfect temperature. "But I don't want to excel at school if it means staying away from you. It hurts so much thinking that you don't want me."

He sniffs. "Owen, I do, I swear," he whispers.

I wipe a tear from his eye. "Then let's do this right. Clay Cannon, do you want to be my boyfriend, feeding or no feeding? But I'm warning you, I might get clingy and want to hop into bed with you every night."

We both snicker. "But your parents—"

"Answer the question, baby."

He nods. "I want you so much, Owen Bhat. So, yes. But if—" His words are cut off by my mouth on his. For the first time in my life, I'm not overthinking the consequences. I'm following my heart, and he's right here, holding me in a perfect embrace.

We break apart and I gaze into the vampire's gorgeous eyes. Clay strokes my face and grins. "So we're really doing this? Even despite your parents?"

I nod. "I think I may have a plan to help us out. But we'll need to call in some favors to do it."

It's the next morning, and I'm occupying an entire corner of tables at Mummy Mocha, courtesy of Seth. Kovi and Tanner managed to get me a big-screen TV setup from a librarian gorgon. Our plan is well underway, and I'm trying to even out my breathing. When my phone buzzes in my pocket, I'm broken from my self-meditation.

MOM

We are parking now. We want to hear your big announcement.

Well, there goes my Zen. My pulse rises when I think about all of the planning we did last night and early this morning. "What if this doesn't work and they still hate me?" I click on my laptop, and fear and panic fill my veins. *What if this is all for nothing?*

"Owen..." Clay says, rubbing my arm.

"What if...my parents hate me forever and abandon me?" My throat goes dry, and my vision blurs. Oh boy, the panic attack is taking over. My breath becomes shallow, and I try to slow it down, to no avail. "Oh monster god..." I rasp.

"Hey, hey, no," Clay says firmly. He gently turns me toward him and puts both hands on my deltoids. "Owen, look at me," he murmurs.

I glance up to see this beautiful vampire face inches from mine. "Focus on me," Clay whispers. My vision clears, and when he puts his forehead on mine, I shut my eyes. I focus on his skin and the scent of his mouth. "Breathe with me."

I do as I'm told. The hurricane in my heart dies down, but not because of any visualization exercises. It's Clay—feeling him put his hands on my neck and gently massage me brings me back down to Earth. The spot where his head touches mine is everything right now.

Grounding me in the here and now. I breathe slower, in and out. I pay attention to his voice. His presence.

And after a few moments, the panic is gone.

"This is going to work."

"Okay," I reply. "Thank you."

"Anytime, handsome." He winks and grows his fangs, and I

giggle. He's so sexy, but we didn't get intimate last night. I had a lot of work to prepare for this morning's impromptu event, after all. I can ask him to sink his teeth into me another time.

I click my presentation and confirm that I'm displaying it on the big screen. After a moment, I notice two familiar figures approaching the front counter. My parents are already staring at me and Clay, and only turn away when Seth greets them with a charming smile.

"There they are. Shoo," I whisper.

In a blur, Clay uses his vampire speed to dart out of one of the exits of Mummy Mocha. In a flash, he reappears on the opposite side of the café. He's hiding his face behind some random book and he's now sitting with Kovi and Tanner. I need to get used to having a boyfriend with super-hearing.

Monster boyfriend. I love the sound of that.

Two minutes later, my parents greet me with a hug. They each sit and begin to sip their mummy chai drinks. "What's all this, Owen?" Mom asks, pointing at the screen.

"It's about my future." I stand up and start the HowlerPoint presentation. "Now, the following is my current transcript, as well as my GPA."

I point at the screen where all my A's and credits line up. "As you can see, I'm still getting a 4.0."

"Oh, very good." Mom is utterly impressed. She exchanges a look with Dad, who simply nods.

"Now, with these credits, I can go to any prolific human medical school, a process I will begin in August." I click and show images of various classic medical schools.

"Excellent," Mom remarks.

"However, with these credits, I can also major in Monster Medical studies." I click to show a stock image of a doctor woman interviewing a dryad. She's wearing a lab coat, and he's sitting in a large procedure chair.

"Owen," Mom says, her mood souring.

"Please, Mom. Hear me out," I plead. I click and show various headlines of doctors in America garnering accolades for treating monsters. "There is an increasing need for monster medicine. Here are the listings for residencies for monster clinics versus human clinics." The next slide shows the information side by side. "As you can see, there is a demand for monster health. And I want to be part of it. Which is why I'm asking you to reconsider your stance on funding my medical school endeavors. With my grades, I've proven my future is a worthwhile investment." I click to show a stock image of a sack of money and the words "The End."

I hold my breath and, at long last, turn to my parents. Dad has his arms crossed with his unreadable expression, and Mom just looks confused. She turns to Dad and says, "Talk some sense into your son."

Dad clears his throat and studies me. "What would you do if we said no, Owen?"

I glance away at Clay, his wide eyes peeking above the book in his hands. "I'll go anyway and take whatever scholarships I can get. My grades speak for themselves."

Dad nods, and Mom sighs. "Beta, we know your grades are good. We know you'll learn as much as you can about whatever species you set your mind to. We're just worried about all these monsters. Since you're not one of them, how will you be protected if they want to, I don't know, eat your blood?"

I open my mouth to speak, but I immediately feel a presence at my side. "I'll protect him."

I glance at Clay next to me. He's beaming at my folks with his fangs out—this was not part of the plan. "It takes a monster to stop a monster, amiright?"

He chuckles, but my parents just stare at him in shock.

"Young man, you told us yesterday you want to devour our son!" Mom says.

Clay simply looks at me and shifts his fangs in. "It has taken me years to control my hunger for blood, but I do it every day. I don't feed on humans regularly, and certainly not without their consent. But if I ever do anything to threaten him, I give Owen full permission to use a wooden stake on my heart if I try anything funny. Meanwhile, I'll make it my life's mission to support your son." He wraps his arm around me. "I have a vested interest in him, until we're old and gray. He'll be an amazing doctor, and I'll protect him the entire time."

I caress his face, then turn to my folks. They watch us quietly with neutral faces, and sip their drinks. Then, they stand up. My heart pounds in my chest. Dad walks closer to Clay and places his hand on my boyfriend's shoulder.

"I saw you five minutes ago. My son...he has panic attacks."

"Dad, I'm right here," I mutter.

"And you could have eaten him just now, but instead, I watched you calm him down."

"He did?" Mom murmurs.

"Owen loves the monsters," Dad says. His eyes dart from me back to Clay. "And you might be good for him."

Clay and I share looks of pleasant surprise.

"But if you hurt my son, I'll bring the stake to you," Dad says.

"And if you distract him from his monster medical studies, I'll do the same," Mom adds.

I shake my head in bewilderment. "What?"

Dad shrugs. "We could never stop you from studying what you wanted." He waves at the big screen. "Clearly, you've laid out why being a monster doctor is important to you. And lucrative."

"We just wanted you to be safe. But you've made connections to the monster community. You seem to have found one who can treat you right," Mom says.

I gulp and nod. "Um, exactly."

"Under my protection, Owen will become the best doctor ever," Clay says, squeezing my hand.

Dad and Mom give each other satisfied nods, then lean closer to hug me.

"Have a good week, son," Dad says.

"Don't be a stranger!" Mom adds.

"Bye, guys," I say.

Before they leave, Mom points to Clay. "We would love to find out why our son is so smitten with you. We'll be seeing you over the summer and at Thanksgiving, yes?"

Clay gives her a stunned nod, and with that, my parents are gone.

"What...what does that mean?" Clay asks in a whisper.

I grin and pull him in by his hips. I peck him on the lips and say, "I think that means, welcome to the Bhat family, vampire."

We giggle and kiss, right there in a corner of Mummy Mocha while Kovi, Tanner, and Seth cheer. How can I care about my friends giving me a hard time? My parents are cool with my monster studies, and more importantly, I have Clay in my arms. I'm truly a lucky guy.

CHAPTER
NINETEEN
CLAY

"'mon babe," I say, throwing an arm over his shoulders and steering Owen toward his dorm room. I do my best to refrain from inhaling his sweet vanilla-nutmeg scent, but I fail. "If we don't get a move on, we'll miss the group."

"Right." With a last glance around, where he grabs his phone and keys—I can learn a lot from Owen—he picks up his overnight bag, and we take off, holding hands. I've already stashed my duffle in my car, so before we get to the stairs, I make Owen pass over his bag, which he does with little protest. I like to spoil my guy.

Owen and I walk across campus to the parking lot. It's a warm and sunny late spring day, with the trees leafed out in that vibrant yellow-green they get in Pennsylvania. The zombies have planted flower boxes and hung flowering baskets on some of the light posts, so the whole school looks really pretty and smells very bright and floral.

While of course the nature spirits—water spirits, tree folk, fae—are out in full force enjoying the sunshine, other monsters won't be outdone. At least five werewolves are in a circle in the quad playing Cards Against Monsterkind, and a phoenix zooms past us overhead. Plenty of humans mill about too, talking with friends and scrolling on their phones.

Owen tilts up his head to watch the phoenix. Funny how flying used to be such a hurdle for me. He gives me a shy smile. "Thanks for inviting me along."

I roll my eyes. "Of course I'm inviting you along. You're my boyfriend."

And I'm in love with you. I want to spend every moment of every day with you. I want you to be my partner in life. I don't want to do anything without you.

I can't say any of that out loud, though. Can I?

We get in my car and drive through the school gates, past the gargoyles. I wave at the one who's alive. He gives me an up-nod with his chin.

I spend most of the drive to Stokerbram Park lost in my thoughts. How can I tell Owen my feelings? Should I just do it? Blurting things out is often the way I end up going through life, but with him ... I wish it could be more romantic.

I'm pretty sure he cares about me, but love? I'm not sure about that.

We arrive at the park and join a group of vampires gathered at the trailhead.

"Hey," I say, waving like a dork.

"Clay! Good to see you!" Shannon says, coming over to give me a hug. I return it lightly, but I swear I hear Owen growl. So I kiss his cheek, and his shoulders relax. "And you brought your feeder," she continues, sweeping out a hand to indicate Owen.

"We're actually just boyfriends," I correct, taking Owen's hand. "The status of us feeding is personal, if you don't mind."

Shannon raises both eyebrows. "I, uh, apologize. You're right."

"All good," I say.

The thrill, the anticipation of going gliding fills me. While before, it brought on nothing but dread, now it's just...fun.

"Where's a good place to watch you?" Owen asks, swiveling his head around. "Maybe I could go up to one of the lookout points—"

"Do you want to go flying with me?" I blurt.

"Wha-what?" Owen stutters. "Like, in the air?"

I smirk. "Yes. I generally fly in the air. You taught me, you should know that."

He slugs my shoulder gently and looks down at his body. "But aren't I too heavy?"

"Monster strength." I point at my biceps. "It'll be fun. Come on."

"That's so cute you take your boyfriend with you," Shannon says. "If only Raymond would do something that romantic."

Awesome. I'm being romantic.

Ray walks over. "I'm not romantic?"

"I mean," Shannon says, putting a hand on her hip, "you could be *more* romantic."

Ray raises an eyebrow. "I'll show you *romantic*. Just you wait." He puts an arm around her waist and walks away with her.

I turn back to Owen. "You don't have to go with me, but I wanted to show you how far I've progressed."

While he's pursing his lips and seeming a little wary, it doesn't take long before he smiles. "I trust you. Okay, you can carry me. And you're right. Remember when you first started out? How hard it was?"

"I'm always hard for you," I mumble into his ear as I tug him closer by his waist.

"Haha. I know."

"But yeah," I say, my tone changing to serious. "I know.

Thanks for helping me figure out how to fly. I don't think I would've ever gotten the nerve to try without your support."

"Ready?" Shannon calls. And she lunges into the air, catching a breeze easily.

I pick Owen up, and while I want to carry him like a bride, I think he may kill me if I do that. So instead, I just sort of hold him at my side, my arm slung under his armpits, as I press him to me.

He looks terrified: eyes blown wide open, body frozen, lips parted.

"I got you," I murmur, and he nods, clenching my waist with his legs.

Taking everything I've learned into account, I sense the shift in my body to go into flight mode.

Ready.

I bend my legs and spring up.

Immediately, I find a gust of air, and we're soaring up over the trees.

Together.

"You okay?" I ask Owen, as his dark curls tangle around his face.

"Yeah," he says, his voice an octave higher than usual.

So I hold him tighter as we fly past the waterfall and over down into the gorge. We zoom by some rock outcroppings.

I glance around, surveying the pretty, wooded scenery.

Let's go to the river.

Owen relaxes in my arms, and while I'm not loosening my hold on him by any means, at least he doesn't have a death grip on me.

I whip us between the trees, gliding down to almost touch the river, and get sprayed by the mist from the whitewater rapids. Then we sail up on a gust of wind past the tops of the trees.

"Holy shit! This is fun!" Owen crows, his eyes alight behind his glasses and his mouth in a wide grin.

I ride a thermal up into a spiral, and as I do, I kiss him. We're soaring midair, and nothing could be better than holding my boyfriend in my arms and feeling his warmth next to me as he trusts me.

Our lips meet, our tongues touch, and our kiss is searing.

He opens his mouth to say something, but I need to pay attention. He seems to get the message fast, and I take us to a rocky ledge at the side of the waterfall, where we land softly.

"Wow, that was such a rush!" Owen says, breathless.

"Right? It's almost as good as sex."

Almost as good as *feeding on someone during* sex.

Owen leans in to kiss me again, and it's a slow, leisurely kiss. Deep and warm and soft. My hands grip his hips, then slide down to palm his ass.

He moans into me, his glasses fogging up.

That moan does something to my restraint. Now I'm kissing him hard, our tongues battling for dominance, my dick getting hard and pressing into the front of his jeans, where I can tell he's hardening too.

"Monster god, Clay, I want you."

"Out here?" I mumble against his lips.

"Yes, here."

I take a step back and survey where we are. Mist from the waterfall sprays us, and the breeze ruffles the pine trees, but otherwise, it's quiet. My monster senses aren't picking up on any vampires close by. Maybe they all went in the other direction.

"Okay," I whisper and move us so he's facing the waterfall. I come up behind him and lick along his neck. The soft skin behind his ears is particularly arousing.

I rub my cock against his round, firm ass. My arms wrap

around his waist like steel bands, holding him to me. My hand slides down his body to stroke his cock, which is hard against his zipper.

With a flick, I unbutton his jeans and reach into his underwear to grip his hot, velvety length. The tip is leaking, and I use the precum to stroke him a few times.

"I want you to feed off of me," Owen blurts, pressing his ass into me.

My fangs descend. Every nerve ending in my body goes on alert. A powerful sense of *want* courses through me.

I've been tamping down the siren call of Owen's hot blood the entire time we've been together. He makes me so thirsty in so many ways.

But...it's inherently dangerous for me to feed from my boyfriend. I'd be sucking his blood, his life force, and they told us in anatomy class that humans need blood to function. Okay, I already knew that.

What would happen if I drank too much? If I couldn't stop?

What if I got lost in the moment and didn't realize that I was taking too much from him? What if I took too much from my lover because feeding from him is all about me? Although humans can also get off on it too, so maybe that's not totally true.

I open my mouth to argue, but Owen twists around and puts a finger over my lips. "I know the risks. But I trust you."

I should argue with him more. That'd be the right thing to do.

But I also know that I care about this man so much that there's no way that I would let myself hurt him.

Which means...oh, monster god. Which means that this is going to be hot.

"Okay," I whisper. "Just stop me if you don't want to do it anymore."

"Deal."

The waterfall pounds right next to us as I kiss his lips and shove Owen's pants down to mid-thigh, then spin him around so his back's to my front. Then I quickly undo my pants, releasing my hard cock.

I spit on my hand and use it and his precum to pump his dick while I slot my cock between his legs.

Intercrural sex is awesome.

Owen wiggles under me, clearly trying to get me to bite him, as he pushes his neck toward my mouth.

Pushing his shirt to the side, I trace a path with my tongue from his ear to his shoulder, then murmur, "You ready?"

"Yes. Do it."

"You need something to brace against." Using my monster speed, I yank off my shirt and put it between him and a smooth rock, so he has a padded surface to lean against. "That's better."

He reaches over his shoulder. "Clay. Do. It."

With a delicious inhale, I puncture his skin and sink my fangs into his neck.

Immediately, my mouth floods with his copper-tinged blood.

Oh, monster fucking heaven.

In the world of out-of-body experiences, there's the release from orgasm, and then there's this: a delirium I've never felt before, because I've never fed on anyone I've had feelings for—at least not feelings like this.

His hot blood pumps into my mouth, filling me with his life force, his essence, and I'm enraptured by it.

But not so enraptured that I forget to get him off.

I stroke his cock faster, focusing on the tip, doing a little twist at the end, and I thrust between his legs, my movements artless as I continue to feed on his delicious blood.

I'm about to fall to my knees in front of him when Owen

starts coming, and his orgasm triggers a change in his blood. His hot cum spills all over my hand.

I *feel* him coming—as if I'm the one having his orgasm, not him—as I suck his blood, and with a hiss, I pull back from him, needing to not take too much.

I'm about to come myself when Owen drops to his knees and takes my cock in his mouth. It doesn't take me many thrusts before I'm releasing—the rush as strong as this waterfall swollen with snowmelt.

I've never felt more sated.

It takes both of us a moment to come down from our highs, and then I go over to a small pool of water and wash my hands, cleaning up as best as I can and helping Owen do the same.

"Shit," I whisper, looking at the bruised skin on his neck. "I hurt you."

"You did not. I loved it."

I kiss his neck with my mouth open, so the healing nature of my saliva will speed along his healing. And also so it doesn't look like he's in high school with a big hickey.

"Feeling a little better?" I ask.

"Yeah." His voice is husky.

We adjust our clothes back to normal, then sit on the rock outcropping, our legs dangling over the side. The entire gorge spreads out before us, and in the far distance, I can make out other members of the gliding group catching thermals.

Owen snuggles against me, and I wrap an arm around his shoulders. He rests his head on my torso.

My heartbeat starts going a mile a minute.

Better just do it.

"Owen, I have to tell you something."

"What is it?"

"I've been young for a long time, and I'm going to be alive for quite some time still. But being immortal means nothing without you. I didn't start living until you found me. I'm really, really in love with you."

He sucks in a sharp breath and pushes up his glasses, looking up at me. "Yeah?"

"Absolutely."

Owen gives me a devastating smile. "It's a good thing, since I'm in love with you, too."

TWENTY

OWEN

I walk down the path to the river with a throng of fellow students. Monsters and humans of all kinds amble away from campus as the sun sets. It feels like I'm in a parade with various spider shifters, werebears, mummies, and so many other species, along with my fellow humans. I smile, content to know that this is my community now. Nine months ago, we were all at an off-campus riverbank bonfire to start the year, and now we're here, two weeks before the end of the semester. With the glow of the firelight and crowd of happy students, this is the perfect environment to bookend my first full academic year here at the infamous Creepin U.

After several minutes, we're all drinking libations by the fire. It's a warm spring night and music and laughter fill the air. Shonda regales me with hilarious stories of her study sessions with a cyclops and a gnome, and Rachel and I howl with laughter. The smell of woodfire, carefully controlled by the phoenixes, fills my nostrils, and I couldn't be more content.

Of course, so much of that is because of a certain special someone. I peer in the distance at the monster jocks splashing around the river. We college students will take any excuse to take off our clothes during a party, but they genuinely seem to be having fun. I came with my boyfriend, but he was quickly whisked away by his team. Only now I don't see him...

"Boo!" I turn and giggle at the voice next to me. A dripping wet, shirtless Clay is the best kind of Clay—tied with every other version of my man.

"Hey, you." I beam at him and hand him my cup.

He grins and sips the beer. His long dark locks are soaking wet, evidence of his romp in the river, and he resembles a big, wet puppy.

"Wow, Owen. When you said back in January that you wanted a vampire boyfriend, I didn't think you'd successfully manifest it," Rachel remarks. Shonda chuckles, and I shrug. My friends have all since met Clay as my significant other, and I have no qualms touting him as my man across campus.

"Hey, I've seen the presentation," Clay says. "More like, open invitation."

Shonda and Rachel laugh, but I simply grin. "That was a general presentation, in reference to any queer vampire boy." I take back the drink. "But you fit the bill adequately."

"*Adequately*?" Clay makes a dramatic face, but my friends and I crack up. "I'll have you know I am pretty fly."

"For a vampire guy," I add. I wink and begin to wrap my arm around him, then remember he's dripping wet. "Do you need a towel, babe?"

"Nah." He shakes his body and head aggressively, like a golden retriever. My friends and I get sprayed and shout, all while Clay laughs. "I can take care of it."

"Aw, okay, with that, we're leaving," Shonda says through a giggle.

"Yeah. Come on, I think Kovi is letting people swing off his branches." Rachel nudges Shonda then points away. In the distance, I can make out Tanner standing next to his tall, tree-monster boyfriend. His arm branches are spread as folks attempt to leap up to him. I'm glad the two of them are still going strong despite their contentious love story. And I'm even more happy I have a love of my own.

With the girls gone, I pull Clay closer, wetness be damned. "If I didn't love you, these water antics would be ridiculous," I say with a grin.

"Yeah, but you still think I'm fly." His grin drops. "Do kids nowadays say fly?"

"No," I murmur against his lips. We kiss and then break apart with a laugh. No one makes me smile as much as Clay Cannon.

After a moment, I gaze up to see several thunderbirds and vampires flipping around in the sky. Their aerial acrobatics are impressive, and students are cheering and howling at them. I recognize some of them as Clay's friends from the Vampire Gliding Enthusiasts, so I look down at my boyfriend.

"You wanna go join them?"

"Should I?"

I shrug. "The semester's essentially over. It's a party. And it looks fun."

He seems to mull it over, then grins with his fangs out. "Be right back." He pecks me on the cheek, and, with supernatural speed, dashes up a tree. Less than a minute later, he's gliding over the bonfire, laughing with his fellow vampires. He does multiple spins and somersaults as he and the other vampires land on opposite trees. They launch themselves off, ping-ponging back and forth through the skies. Seeing him fly is a sight to behold, and knowing how far he's come warms my soul.

To think I tried to resist falling for this bloodsucker.

I shake my head and grin, then take a sip. After a minute, I notice one person in the crowd walking up to me with purpose.

He's holding a bundle of cloth in his arms. Between his serious face and his brisk walking, my anxiety rises.

"Yuki?"

"You. Owen Bhat. Where is Clay?"

The dude's voice sounds sterner and louder than I've ever heard him. The last I heard, he outright refused to join the end-of-year student bonfire, opting to stay in the dorm.

"He's um...up there." We both look up at the aerial theatrics.

"Well then, you can take care of this."

"What?" I ask.

He pushes the bundle toward me and I put down my drink to take it. I recognize it as one of Clay's sleeping shirts. When I open it, a black furball launches out.

"Woah!" I stumble back, only to have it land on my shoulder. Then, the critter licks my neck.

I gasp. "Bat Nathanson!" I almost tear up in joy. I take my baby in my hand, and he smiles at me. "You're back!"

"He is," Yuki says, unimpressed. The two of us walk while I cradle my familiar in my arms. Not only do I recognize his cute little rodent face, but he's still wearing the pink scarf Clay made for him. "He kept rapping at our window. I let him fly in because it was really annoying."

"When?" I can't stop smiling as we walk away from the crowd and bonfire and toward the riverbank.

"Maybe half an hour ago. It was very disturbing." Yuki seems genuinely vexed as he shoves his hands into his hoodie pocket. "But I know he's your familiar. I could tell he was looking for you. He landed on Clay's shirt. If I hadn't forcibly brought him here, he'd be squeaking and flapping at me all evening. I figured..."

I cuddle my fur baby closer. "Well, thank you, Yuki."

When I look up, Clay descends from the sky. "Yuki?"

"Look who turned up at your dorm!" I exclaim.

Clay gasps and moves closer. "Our baby!"

"Yeah, you're welcome," Yuki says in a bored tone.

Clay snickers as he rubs BN's belly. "Well thank you, man. I know how annoying you think parties are. You can go now. You're officially relieved of your roommate-ly duties."

"Yes, well parties don't fit well with me, so I should..." His words trail off. While Clay cuddles BN, I notice Yuki staring out at the riverbank. When I track his gaze, I notice some water polo monsters are still bouncing around a beach ball and laughing.

Yuki clears his throat but doesn't turn away from the riverbank. "I'm already here. I...I guess I could stick around."

I bite back a laugh; I know all too well what it's like to be enthralled by monster jocks despite myself. "Well, I hope you find this gathering of the student body to be...enlightening."

He bristles and walks away. He's a perceptive dude, that Yuki, but he's not very good at hiding what he desires. He's ambling toward the riverbank for crying out loud.

I turn back to Clay and BN. My boyfriend wipes his tears as our familiar licks his hand. I rub his bare shoulder and smile at him. "Wow," he whispers.

"I know. We must have done something right, eh? Bat Nathanson is back, presumably forever."

"He missed the blood bottle." Clay won't stop crying. "That's probably all it is. He doesn't actually care about us."

I laugh as my eyes begin to burn. I move closer and gaze at our pet smiling up at us. "Well, I read that familiars have an emotional connection with their witches, and I suppose that's us." We both chuckle. "What do you think he's thinking?"

Clay looks up at me, tears streaming down his gorgeous face. "He's thinking...he used to be so lonely. He didn't think anyone would understand him, or support him, or give him space to learn how to fly." Clay sniffs, and his words clench around my heart. "And now he gets to feel love for the first time instead of vapid emptiness."

Well damn. I lean forward and slowly kiss Clay, holding his face in place. When I pull back, I wipe his cheek of another tear. "I bet he's thinking that he's always wanted a jock that understands him for all his nerdy quirks. And that you've shown him how amazing it is to love and be loved by a monster. And he has no intention of looking for anyone else." I lean forward to kiss Clay again, when—

"Squeak!" I look down at our familiar, cradled against Clay's chest. We laugh, then he flies up and lands on my shoulder

"I can't believe Bat Nathanson felt all that," Clay says with a wry grin. He wipes his eyes and I snicker.

"Well, he's so damn in love with you. And so am I."

Clay touches my face. "I love you, too, Owen," he whispers. I make a mental note to never let go of this vampire man. Come hell or high water, I want to ride with him and be the love of his life.

Instead of saying any of that, I reach up to my left shoulder and pick up BN. I hear a gasp, and then look up.

"Is that who I think it is?" Shonda nearly squeals as she approaches us. Rachel, Tanner, and Kovi—in human form now —all stride toward us.

"Have you guys met our familiar?" Clay asks. We take turns passing around our pet. Everyone coos and fawns over him, and our familiar basks in all the attention.

I gaze at my amazing boyfriend, and his face glows in the firelight. Here, in this moment, I have so much more than I could have dreamed of when I first arrived at Creelin nine months ago. And I wouldn't have it any other way.

TWENTY-ONE

"Be a good bat and do what Kovi and Tanner say." Owen drops a kiss on Bat Nathanson's fuzzy black forehead. BN blinks and nuzzles into him.

"We'll be back soon," I assure BN, tickling under his chin as Owen passes the tiny creature to Tanner.

Our baby squeaks. I'm getting pretty good at telling what his squeaks mean, and this one is a blasé "so long, see ya."

Teenager. He's getting so big. And he adores Kovi and Tanner, who are watching him for our date night.

It's a week after the bonfire night. Summer's going to be annoying without Owen, and I'm going to miss him. But I hope he agrees to my big surprise for fall.

Keep it together, Clay.

"Here's his bag," I say, handing Kovi a tote with BN's bottles of blood, his tiny stuffed animal toy, blankets, and other essentials. Even teens need their toys.

"Don't worry about a thing," Tanner says, running a finger over BN's head. BN closes his eyes, enjoying the touch. "We'll take care of him."

"And you can FangChat him if you really want," Kovi adds. "We'll be around."

Owen exhales. "Okay, good." He bites his lip and shifts his weight from one leg to the other. "So, where are we going?"

"It's a surprise," I say, hooking my arm around his neck.

Instead of driving, I fly him to downtown Creelin.

"First stop, dinner," I say.

"Cannon, where are we going?" Owen repeats, looking at all the different restaurants on this street.

"If you're up for it, we could go to the Indian one we went to with your parents—and try to create a new memory."

He shakes his head. "They don't have anything for you to eat there."

"I'm good, and I can fill up at the next place we go," I say.

Owen studies my face. "If you insist."

But I've watched how he is in the cafeteria and can tell he wants some traditional food. "I think you'd like the dal soup and chicken monster-sala."

His stomach rumbles. I kiss him. "Come on."

I drag him inside.

After he eats his fill, a happy smile on his face, we go back outside into the last light of the day.

"Where next?"

"Another surprise," I say.

We go down the street and walk a few blocks over to get in line at Scareoke.

"Karaoke?" Owen says, chuckling. "Can you sing?"

"Nope," I say cheerfully. "But that doesn't stop me from trying."

As the line moves slowly up, we get to the werewolf bouncer. Oh, shit, did I forget my wallet again?

I pat my pockets, but Owen's pulling out his wallet and he hands me my ID.

"When did you take to carrying this around for me?"

He shrugs. "It seemed like the best way to help you."

I kiss his temple. "Thanks."

I show the bouncer my ID, Owen shows his, and I pay the cover charge for both of us. We step inside, and Brandon is waving at us frantically.

"He's over there," I say, gesturing. "Bran adores karaoke."

"Is he good at it?"

"Nope, but the nøkk makes up for it. Steve's voice is outstanding."

Owen gives me an unreserved smile. "I can't wait."

We slide in the circular booth next to Brandon and Steve.

"So glad you could make it!" Bran chirps. Steve gives us a small smile, which for him is a full-on belly laugh.

We order drinks. I get a blood martini, which is just blood served in a martini glass. A few more members of the water polo team—Nick, Phil, and Ren—join us.

And then it's our turn for karaoke.

Brandon, of course, is first, and he gets up there with Steve to sing "Space Oddity" by David Bowie. Naturally, Bran's ground control and the nøkk is Major Tom.

Then Phil, the sasquatch, saunters up and brings down the house with "New York, New York," Frank Sinatra style. That kid really should be singing for a major record label.

Nick gets up and sings "I'm Gonna Be (500 Miles)" by The Proclaimers—I guess that's a nod to his Scottish background—and then it's my turn.

Little monster butterflies flop around in my stomach as I approach the stage. I peer into the lights, and while it's hard to see at first, I find Owen.

The MC puts on "Come On Get Higher" by Matt Nathanson, and Owen beams widely at me.

Well. I do my best. I'm not a great singer, but what I lack in voice, I make up for in moves.

When I finish the song, I get a huge round of applause and rejoin my friends.

"You're amazing," Owen says. "I love that song."

"Me too." I nuzzle his face. "I love you more, though."

"This is a cool surprise."

"I'm just getting started."

AN HOUR LATER, we're in the common room of Karloff Hall, and Brandon's helping me set up the projector, which is hooked up to my laptop.

Owen's sitting on the squeaky old couch, looking quizzically as the nøkk and Nick put up a screen. A few other friends mill around.

When I finally get the projector focused and working, my HowlerPoint slide presentation pops up.

"*WHY I LOVE OWEN BHAT*," by Clay Cannon.

Owen inhales sharply. Is he going to cry?

I fly over to him—not literally, just using my monster speed. "Hey, are you okay?" I murmur, getting on my knees before him.

He runs a hand through my hair. "Yes, you big brute! You're being all sentimental. Just show me your slides."

I grin, flashing my fangs. "Okay, hang on."

Returning to the computer, I push a button, and the slide changes to one of Owen studying. His face is down, and he didn't know I was sneaking a photo of him.

"The future Doctor Bhat is the smartest person I know," I begin.

"What about me?" Bran calls.

"You're pretty," I say. "And yes, you're smart, but ..."

"I'm just teasing," Brandon says. "Owen is the smartest."

Owen's face is thoroughly heated.

Later. You can feed on him later.

I move to the next slide, and it's a photo of us and Bat Nathanson between us. "Owen is the most caring bat dad I've ever met."

"Does Clay know any other bat dads?" the nøkk whispers to Brandon.

"It doesn't matter," Bran whispers back. I puff out my chest. This is why Bran's my best friend.

The next slide is a photo of me flying, which Owen took and posted on his Fangstagram. "Owen's taught me so much about so many different things. He taught me how to fly."

"You didn't know how to do that?" someone calls.

"Nope," I admit. "I couldn't do it until he helped."

"That's so cool," Bran says, giving Owen an up-nod.

Next slide is a picture of me with a bunch of books. "He taught me monster anatomy," I say.

"I would've thought you had a Ph.D, in that already," Nick calls.

I tut. "Leave me alone, I'm being sentimental."

Everyone laughs. Owen is smiling.

The next slide is a photo of me, shirtless in bed—one that Owen took after sex.

"Wait, why did you share the hot photo of you?" Brandon asks.

"I mean, wouldn't you?" I counter.

Bran laughs. "Okay, fair."

"Oh my monster god, I can't believe you're sharing that!" Owen shrieks, covering his face with his hands and peeking through his fingers.

"But I look good," I say, tilting my head.

Dropping his hands, Owen rolls his eyes. "True. You do."

The next photo is one of his family. "He's a loving son—"

I keep going. Finally, at the end, I say, "Owen Bhat, you're the best thing that ever happened to me, and I want to know if you'd like to move in with me the next school year. It'd save on housing fees."

Nick snorts. "Sure, it's a budgetary issue."

But Owen's eyes are bright. "I'd love to move in with you," he whispers.

"I'm so glad we were lab partners," I say, and kiss him.

EPILOGUE

OWEN

(A FEW SHORT YEARS LATER)

The spring sun is shining but my head is spinning. No amount of coffee is going to compensate for the fact that I did another all-nighter. I walk into my apartment, put away my lab coat, and take off my red scrub shirt. After I toss it into the bathroom hamper, I amble through the living room area. Our little studio apartment isn't much, but it's home for the three of us. A wooden partition separates the bed from the rest of the space. In the corner, Bat Nathanson's terrarium sits atop a tiny desk and is covered in a yellow blanket. I peek under—yup, he's still sleeping, and the newspaper lining on the bottom is fresh and clean.

I smile, then yawn and scratch my chest through my tank top. I amble to the kitchen, all at once starving, dizzy, and loopy. One would think that after several months of nighttime hospital shifts for my residency, I'd become nocturnal, like my familiar. But alas, I am not, so the room spins while I open the fridge door.

I grunt after looking through our paltry selection. I know

it's the lack of sleep talking, but I would give up my arm for a werebear claw from Mummy Mocha right now. I wonder if we have any more boxes of Blob Tarts. Or Rice Harpy's Treats?

And where's Clay, anyway?

Just while thinking that, my boyfriend walks through the door. He's all sweaty, fresh from a run, and his arms are exposed in his black tank top over gray sweatpants. He's the hot jock vampire of my dreams, as always, but I'm too sleepy to care about that.

His face lights up, fangs out, when he realizes I'm there. "Hey, Dr. Bhat."

I give a feeble smile and shut the door. "Not a doctor yet," I murmur. I fill up a cup with water and he approaches me.

"Well, I got a gift, but it's only for a doctor after a hard night at work." He approaches me with a grin.

I snicker despite myself. "Well this almost-doctor is about to pass out, so you'd better make it quick."

He kisses my cheek from behind. "Oh no, don't want that." He pulls me toward the brown kitchen table and forces me to sit. "Do you want to sleep or have breakfast?" He places a crinkled paper bag on the counter and I smile.

"I want to do both," I say in a tired voice. "But thank you."

"Of course. Eat up, you need your strength."

"Yeah, so you can have my precious hemoglobin." Opening up the bag, I reveal a flaky round pastry. "A cinnamonster bun!"

Clay shrugs. I know he has decelerated aging, but he's just as handsome as he was in undergrad those few years ago. "You deserve it after a long night of helping triage monster patients."

I chomp on the baked good and the sweetness delights me. "You won't believe what this one mummy came in with," I say with a mouth full of pastry.

Clay laughs and we talk for a few minutes more. When I'm done eating, he insists I take the first shower. We have dark blinds, and it's not like Bat Nathanson will disturb me when I nap during the day. My body is putty in his hands when he pushes me toward the bathroom.

"Thank you. For breakfast."

"You're welcome," he says, pushing on my back. "Now go shower so you can sleep."

"Okay, but sleep with me?" I ask through a yawn. I hand him my glasses and make it to the bathroom door.

"Sure, but I'll shower after you because I'm all sweaty. Arms up, Bhat."

I lift up my arms and he strips me of my tank top. With that done, I smile and peck him on the lips. "You're such a helpful vampire," I murmur in my sleepy tone. "You deserve some sex and blood when we're both done showering."

He laughs. "Okay, okay, but go clean up."

My body is on autopilot when I shower. I barely comb my hair before crash-landing on our bed. Clay tells me he's going to bathe, and I tell myself to wake up so we can get frisky. I'm even looking forward to the hot sting of him taking some of my blood. But before I can properly make myself look sexy, the world blanks out.

I WAKE up not sure of what's going on. Sunlight is streaming through our blackout curtains. In the bed next to me, someone is scrolling through their phone—*Clay*.

"Hey," I mutter through a stretch.

"Hey yourself. You feeling better now?"

"Yup." I sit up in bed and notice I'm naked under the covers.

Upon further inspection, it seems Clay is, too. "How long was I out?"

"Four hours." He puts down the phone and leans over to my side. He kisses my forehead and I hum in delight. "But you needed the rest, you big medical resident, you."

"Yeah, we have a huge night ahead of us." I gaze at his toned naked body. Most days I can't believe he's still dating me. I caress his chest, and he smiles.

"We should probably get dressed in a bit."

That wakes me up. "Oh, I think we have time." In a blur, I pounce on him. Clay giggles in surprise as I straddle him. "As I recall, I owe you some sex."

"Owen, sex isn't transactional. You know that—" I cut his words off with a kiss. He massages my mouth like it was made for him. When I pull back, his eyes are brimming with lust.

"When was the last time you had some blood, huh?" I trace his lip with my finger.

"Um, I think yesterday I had a bag, but—"

"No, no," I purr. "When was the last time you got it from the source?"

His brow furrows. "Owen, you don't have to—"

"Oh, but I want to. What's the fun of being with a vampire if he can't take a little bit of my plasma?" I lean in and kiss his neck.

"Yeah, but people will see the fang marks tonight."

I flop back and spread my legs. He eyes me with surprise, but I merely grin at him. "Not if you take it from somewhere..." I pull my balls down and massage my inner groin. My dick hardens at the thought of that pain so close to my ass. "...discreet."

Clay's eyes flare with more heat and he rolls over to me. "Are you sure?" he murmurs against my neck. Despite asking for permission, he proceeds to kiss down my chest.

"Yes...yes," I rasp. I stroke myself, and my hips buck up.

"You can tell me to stop at any time." He reaches my groin and maneuvers me around. Now, Clay's off the bed, and my cock is right at eye level with him. I bend my knees, and he gently supports my thighs.

"Okay, okay, sure." I nod vigorously, staring at our ceiling.

"You really want this, right?"

"Yes," I rasp. I look down, and he licks my scrotum.

"Ah!" I hiss. I instinctively grab my hardness and stroke it. I try not to jerk too much, but Clay is driving me wild with anticipation. I need that vampire pain and pleasure.

"I'm gonna feast on you now, baby." I look down to see him bearing his fangs. "You ready?" I smile and nod, and my hand on my cock stills.

"You're mine," he murmurs. He licks at my groin, right where my inner thigh almost meets my ass and balls. He carefully moves my scrotum out of the way and bathes that sensitive skin with his saliva. "Say it."

"I'm yours," I whisper. My eyes flutter closed.

"Keep saying it," he nearly growls. "Chant it, and I'll pierce the skin and take a small helping of your blood, your essence."

"I'm yours," I say in a whine.

"You're my human, Owen."

"I'm yours, Clay. I'm yours. Only yours. Feed on me. I'm yours. I'm yours. I'm—ah!" My chanting is interrupted by a strangled moan escaping my throat and I tense up.

His fangs. They're in my femoral artery. The first three seconds are painful, but knowing it's the love of my life makes me calm. Then the pain turns into exquisite pleasure.

So I stroke. I stroke with his head so close to my cock. The sounds of him slurping me make for the perfect soundtrack. I'm hard and wanting, and working myself gets me there in record time. This is of course, aided by him gently fondling my balls.

He's so firm with his fangs inside me, yet gentle as he works my sac.

"Fuck...fuck...almost..." My voice whines and gets higher. My hips shift up, but his mouth keeps holding me down. A few more fast, firm strokes, and then—

"UGH!" I bite back a bellow as I shoot, letting that intense orgasm out. Meanwhile, I still feel Clay drinking from me. If ordinary orgasms are fireworks, then vampire feeder orgasms are the big bang, birthing their own universe.

I pass out again for another minute, then wake up to see Clay gently holding me. "How you feeling, love?"

I buzz my lips, raise up a thumb, and we both giggle. "Superb. My thigh is numb, but hey that just means it's healing."

"Good to know."

"I may have to do night shift forever if I have that to look forward to," I remark.

"You know I can't feed from you every day." He strokes my cheek and kisses the top of my head.

"I know. You'd sap all my plasma, and I'd probably shrivel up and die." We both laugh and he cuddles me closer.

"I'll never hurt you."

"Nothing wrong with a little pain," I say against his firm chest.

"I made a vow to your parents all those years ago. And I'll keep protecting you."

I smile and lean into him. "I know, baby."

He rubs my back. "We better get going. Don't want to be late for our friends' big day."

"Of course," I reply. "Right after I regain feeling in my leg again."

"Owen!" Shonda rushes up to me and hugs me before I can say a word.

"Shonda!" Clay says as she holds me tight.

I let my friend go and take a step back. "Good to see you!" She hugs Clay, and I take in my old college friend: her hair is in a poofy updo, and she looks regal in her red dress. She perfectly blends in with the rest of us patrons here at a fancy Pennsylvania restaurant. I greet her date, a monster, before the voice to my left grabs my attention.

"Owen! Clay!" Rachel runs up to us and hugs me as well. Half of her head is styled in a buzzcut, and she's donning a dark pantsuit combo. Her date is a female ogre dressed in similar attire. She almost matches Clay and me in our matching dark navy suits.

"The gang's back together!" Shonda says.

"Of course," I say, sipping from my flute of sparkling cider. "I don't think Kovi and Tanner would physically allow me to miss this."

We all laugh and stand around the round table. While it's difficult for us to get together nowadays, I cleared my schedule to witness Kovi and Tanner's nuptials. It was a lovely ceremony indeed, with trees supernaturally decorated with dozens of types of flowers, all towering over us. Now, here we are, thirty minutes later, in the catering hall, enjoying appetizers and drinks.

"And what's this?" Shonda asks.

I tap the towel-covered travel carrier on the chair next to me. "Tanner specifically wanted our adolescent familiar to be present," I explain.

Rachel peers under the towel. "Where is the little rodent?"

"I'll get him," Clay says. He puts down his drink and whistles. In a moment, Bat Nathanson flies and lands on his wrist. With the sun almost set, our bat has been happy to fly around the woods and back into the catering hall. We're fortunate that facilities nowadays are very accommodating to all familiars, including those who can fly.

"Aw!" Shonda coos. "How are you, buddy?"

"Squeak!" he replies. Our pet hops off and lands on Shonda's hands. As she introduces him to the new monsters in the group, I take a moment to gaze at Clay: his dark hair is slicked back and his suit fits him in a gorgeous way. He's just as handsome now as he was back in college. I may have more of a beard and a thicker waist, but Clay remains forever youthful and sexy. He catches me staring and winks, and I roll my eyes. He's ridiculous and endearing, and I love him more and more every day.

TWO HOURS LATER, the newlyweds are done dancing on the linoleum floor. Tanner has been enchanted by his new husband all night, even when Kovi has been in his giant tree form. Another slow song plays, and Kovi waves his giant branches, beckoning the guests to join him in dancing. With BN secure in his carrier, I take Clay by the hand and, without saying a word, guide him to the dance floor.

I place my hands on his shoulders and he holds my hips. In the sparkling lights of the restaurant, the vampire in my arms looks heavenly. Other couples sway around me, but I don't notice any of them.

"How are you feeling?" he asks.

"Great."

"I meant your inner thigh," he whispers.

"It's fine. You always allow me to heal pretty quickly."

"All right. But if you ever think I'm hurting you—"

"I promise, I'll do what Mom told me and shove garlic down your boxer briefs."

We chuckle and continue to sway to the slow, sultry music. "You're always considerate of me, Clay Cannon. That's why I love you."

"Well, you make me happy, Future Dr. Bhat." He grins. "So I'm going to continue making you happy."

"But what if I said I want you to feed on me every day?" I ask with a challenging eyebrow raised.

"I'd make sure your blood levels are okay, and then..." His fangs pop out and he makes a hissing sound. I laugh at the ridiculousness of his face.

"But what if I said I wanted a wedding ten times bigger than this one?"

"Owen Bhat," he says, shrinking his fangs. "I'll give you all the weddings you want, as long as they're with me."

I gasp, then nod. "I...only want to end up with you."

"Then let's do it." He shrugs and smiles. "Let's fly off into the sunset. Just me, you, and Bat Nathanson."

I snicker. "Would you help me achieve my dreams? Make me get higher, like Matt Nathanson says?"

"For you, baby, I'd help you reach the stars."

A strange idea strikes me. "Let's do it," I whisper.

"Huh?" His brow furrows and he drops his hands. Without another word, I pull him to our table and pick up the pet carrier. In a blur, I drag us out the back entrance of the restaurant. The premises is on a ridge overlooking a massive forest and a distant river, and the sun has given way to a darkening azure sky. I open the carrier door and Bat Nathanson pops out.

When I stand up straight, I take both his hands. "I love you, Clay Cannon."

He looks out at the distant forest, then back at me. "I love you, too. But what—"

"Take us into the sky." I put my arms around his neck and crowd him closer. "Fly me away, handsome vampire guy."

He grins and kisses me on the forehead. Then, he pushes off the ground pulling me up with him. The air currents gather around us, and we gradually rise upward. Bat Nathanson squeaks and flaps around us in a circle.

When I look down, the world seems so small and far away. If I fall, I know this vampire will catch me. That's what Clay Cannon has always done to me—swept me off my feet. When building my future with this vampire, the sky's the limit.

For more Creepin U romance, be sure to read *Dryad, Try Again* by CD Rachels and *The Nøkk and the Jock* by Leslie McAdam.

ACKNOWLEDGMENTS

Our thanks to our readers who asked for more Creepin U!

We are grateful to Angela O'Connell for editing and Katy Cuthbertson for proofreading.

From CD:

Thanks to all my Chill Discoursians: every like and share, every supportive email, every private message, every post on the group, and every review helps tremendously. And thanks for everyone who loves Creepin U. Something tells me classes might be opening again soon...

From Leslie:

Thank you every reader who takes a chance on a new-to-them author, and thank you to every reader who stays with us along the way!

ALSO BY CD RACHELS

Other Works by CD

Maritime Monsters

1. When a shark shifter walks out of the ocean and declares the human researcher to be his mate, nothing in their lives will be the same. Read **"Kissing the Shark".**

Single Gamer's Society

1. When Firass needs a fake boyfriend, his best friend's brother comes to his rescue. Get all the sexy seaside shenanigans in "Failing a Bluff Check" (Single Gamer's Society book 1).

2. Two best friends discover a love that was always there. Read Hamadi's story in **"Himbo Takes it All" (Single Gamer's Society book 2).**

3. The gym bro discovers love where he never expected it. Check out Dylan's story in "Gym Bros and Saving Throws" (Single Gamer's Society book 3).

4. When his high school bully turns up, the trajectory of Natie's life will never be the same. Read the finale of the series in "Redraw Your Hand" (Single Gamer's Society book 4).

Artists and Athletes Series

1. What happened when Ravi, the soccer star, was forced to take an art class? Check out **"The Lines We Draw" Artists and Athletes book 1.**

2. What happened when Landon wanted to turn over a new leaf all while taking a dance class? Check out **"The Moves We Make" Artists and Athletes book 2.**

3. What happened when Dominic went to grad school and met his online video game buddy? For the FREE novella on Kindle delivered via BookFunnel check out **"The Games We Love" Artists and Athletes book 2.5**.

4. What happened when the new music professor met the university Facilities Manager and sparks flew between the co-faculty? Read **"The Strings We Play" Artists and Athletes book 3.**

5. What happened when Omar co-directed a theater production that happened to star his best friend's boyfriend's little brother? Read **"The Roles We Own" Artists and Athletes book 4.**

6. Every Halloween, they keep the masks on and let their passions ignite. Read **"The Masks We Wear" (An Artists and Athletes Halloween Novella)** on Kindle.

Formula Q series

1. When Damon, the motorsports star, meets his gorgeous male nurse, he discovers he wants more than winning races for the first time in his life. He wants Rocky, and damn if that isn't the scariest thing he's ever felt. Read "Drive to Thrive".

2. When Berto meets a new queer friend, his whole life is turned upside down. Shift into gear for book 2 **"Drive to Feel Alive".**

3. When an old friend-turned-enemy joins the grid, feelings that never went away will reignite. Get your engines ready for book 3 "Drive Back to You".

Creepin U

1. Check out the shared universe of monsters going to university together with the scariest creatures of all—humans. For your reading pleasure, enjoy "Dryad, Try Again" part of the Creepin U MM monster romance multiauthor series.

Other Works

Workplace enemies end up on blind date vacation together. The sparks fly, but can they keep up the romance when they get back home? Check out **"Stretch Goals and Sweethearts"** part of the Sweetheart Escapes multiauthor series.

ABOUT CD RACHELS

CD Rachels has been coming up with stories since he was little.

First it was fanfiction, then YA queer novels, and now he's moved up to the big leagues of adult MM romance. In 2020 during quarantine, he burned through more male/male romance books than he ever had in the previous 29 years combined.

He believes there aren't enough BIPOC MC's in MM romance, and he's on a mission to change that.

He lives in New York City with the love of his life and is a nurse by trade. If you're reading this, he's honored that you took the time to help support him as a self-published author.

Be the first to hear about all his updates and new releases! Sign up for his newsletter "The Chill Discourse Report" by going onto his website and downloading a FREE novella.

Visit cdrachelsauthor.com

Get all the graphic teasers on Instagram: @cdrachels

Follow/review his works on Goodreads

Check him out on BookBub too

ALSO BY LESLIE MCADAM

IOU Series (lower angst contemporary m/m romance) (also available in German)

Ambiguous (audio narrated by Hamish Long and Kirt Graves)

Studious (audio narrated by Declan Winters)

Delicious (short story)

Oblivious

Curious

Notorious

Ferocious

Creepin U: A Monster Romance Series (shared-world paranormal m/m romance)

The Nøkk and the Jock (audio coming soon)

Pretty Fly for a Vampire Guy (with CD Rachels)

With J.E. Birk and Rachel Ember (holiday m/m/m romance)

ILYBSM

TMI

FASTER series (shared-world sports m/m romance) (also available in Spanish)

Off Track

Runaway Prince Hotel (shared-world royalcore m/m romance)

Prince of the Northwest Forest

Sarina Bowen's World of True North (shared-world contemporary small town m/m romance)

Undone (audio narrated by Iggy Toma and Tim Paige) (also available in Italian)

Unmanageable (audio narrated by Jacob Morgan and Teddy Hamilton)

Albrecht College Series (college m/m romance)

Mixed Motives (short story)

Look for more in this series coming soon!

All American Boy Series (shared-world m/f romance)

Boy on a Train (audio narrated by Desiree Ketchum and James Cavenaugh)

Romantic comedies with Lex Martin (m/f romance)

All About the D (audio narrated by Stephen Dexter and Ava Erickson)

Surprise, Baby! (audio narrated by Jacob Morgan and Muffy Newton)

The Giving You ... series (m/f romance)

The Sun and the Moon (audio narrated by Tor Thom and Charley Ongel)

The Stars in the Sky

All the Waters of the Earth

The Ground Beneath Our Feet (audio narrated by Tor Thom and Charley Ongel)

Love in Translation series (m/f romance) (also available in Hebrew)

Sol

Sombra

Stand-alone novella (m/f)

Lumbersexual (audio narrated by Tor Thom and Charley Ongel)

ABOUT LESLIE MCADAM

Leslie McAdam is a California girl who loves romance and well-defined abs. She lives in a drafty old farmhouse on a small orange tree farm in Southern California with her husband and two children. Leslie's first published book, *The Sun and the Moon*, won a 2015 Watty, which is the world's largest online writing competition. She's gone on to receive additional literary awards and has been featured in multiple publications, including Cosmopolitan.com. Her books have been Top 100 Bestsellers on both Amazon and Apple Books. Leslie is employed by day but spends her nights writing about the people of your fantasies.

Website: https://www.lesliemcadamauthor.com

M/M-only newsletter: http://eepurl.com/hD9a4r